Trade It All

The Barrington Billionaires
Book Three

Ruth Cardello

Author Contact
website: RuthCardello.com
email: Minouri@aol.com
Facebook: Author Ruth Cardello
Twitter: RuthieCardello

Lance Barrington's priority is business, not pleasure. Only one woman has ever been able to turn him inside out: Willa Chambers, his sister's best friend. Forbidden. Scandalous. Unforgettable.

They've spent the last ten years trying to forget one night.

When Willa and Lance are thrown together again, things heat up fast. Loving him almost destroyed her the first time.

This time, will it heal her?

COPYRIGHT

Print Edition

An original work of Ruth Cardello, 2016.

All Rights Reserved. No part of this book may be used or reproduced in any manner whatsoever without written permission from the author, except in the case of brief quotations embodied in critical articles and reviews.

This book is a work of fiction. The names, characters, places, and incidents are products of the writer's imagination. Any resemblance to actual persons, places, events, business establishments or locales is entirely coincidental.

Dedication

This book is dedicated to my sister, Judy.

I still miss you every day.

A Note to My Readers

Hate to say goodbye to your favorite characters? The perfect solution is a **Synchronized Series!** One world. Three authors. Character cross-over. Triple the amount of books. Binge reading at it's best.

Each author's books are full stories you can enjoy individually! But putting them all together weaves an even more pleasurable reading experience.

Books 1-3 available as of July, 2016. Watch for more releases in Barrington Billionaire Synchronized Series.

Chapter One

August, ten years earlier

WILLA CHAMBERS HESITATED at the door of the guest bedroom she and her twin sister, Lexi, were sharing for the week. Their friend, Kenzi Barrington, had invited them to join her family at their beach house on Nantucket Island as an end-of-summer getaway. It wasn't the first time Willa had gone on vacation with the Barringtons, but this weekend was special.

Willa was eighteen and heading off to Acadia University with Lexi and Kenzi in a few weeks. They weren't children anymore. They were confident women following their dreams and, happily, taking their first big steps together.

Willa wanted a solid career somewhere within the artistic community. She had a deep appreciation for creative works in all forms and, although she'd been told she had a natural talent, she kept her aspirations realistic. If she could support the art community in a meaningful way and make a living at it, she'd consider herself a success.

Lexi wanted to be famous. Or rich. Or rich and famous. She didn't care which came first as long as she found her way to both.

Kenzi—well, she was harder to figure out. Her educational choices were based more on emotion than career path. She was already financially set for life. On her twenty-first birthday, she would inherit a large trust fund from a grandfather she said she'd never known. Kenzi didn't talk about her family much, but Willa knew their relationship was strained. Kenzi didn't like to go home without Willa and Lexi with her. They were her buffer. Her sisters. Willa wasn't surprised when Kenzi choose the same university as she and Lexi had. For someone who seemed to have everything, Kenzi clung to their friendship. She said they were her sanity.

Us? Willa smiled ruefully. *Poor Kenzi.*

Lexi joined her at the doorway in a tiny, neon-pink bikini that was barely decent. Her long blonde hair was tied back in a ponytail that flipped back and forth behind her as she shook her head. Her blue eyes turned critical. "You're not coming down to the beach?"

"I am," Willa answered and waved a towel in the air.

Lexi frowned. "Did you forget your bathing suit?"

"I have it on under this." Willa referenced her denim shorts and T-shirt.

Lexi shook her head and laughed. "Of course you do. Come on; Kenzi said to meet her down on the beach. Her brothers arrived late last night and this morning. They're all here, you know. Even Lance." Lexi wiggled her eyebrows suggestively.

Willa blushed. "I know."

"Look at you, pretending you don't care."

Willa gave her sister a playful shove. "I like him. No big deal."

"You don't like him, you *like* him."

Willa rolled her eyes and tried to look cooler than she felt. "Whatever."

"You've had a crush on him for—like forever. Are you ever going to do anything about it?"

"He's Kenzi's brother," Willa said in protest.

"So what?" Lexi flounced beside her. "We're not in high school anymore. Aren't you curious if college guys kiss better?"

I barely know how high school boys kiss. But that wasn't a conversation Willa wanted to have with Lexi. Sometimes it was simply easier to agree. "I guess."

Willa closed her eyes briefly and let herself imagine kissing Lance. He was two years older than them and already in college at MIT. He was a dual major: Applied Mathematics and Architecture. Brilliant. Gorgeous. He was also the reason she had trouble dating. No one could compare. From the first time Lance had visited the boarding school she, Lexi, and Kenzi attended, Willa had been smitten. Lance was naturally confident. He walked into a room and introduced himself as if everyone should know his name. And everyone did. And his eyes. *Oh God, those eyes.* Dark brown until he talked about something he cared about then they went almost black.

Willa sighed. A look from him was enough to bring a flush to most girls' cheeks. Rowing for a college team had given him an enviable chest and arms—muscular, strong, powerful. He was the perfect height at just over six foot. His face? So stunningly chiseled even married women stopped to take a second look. Really there wasn't an inch of him Willa could imagine not being perfect. She'd spent a significant amount of time imagining it.

And he was downstairs.

Lexi shot her a cheeky grin. "He's hot. If you don't want him, maybe I'll give him a go."

Willa froze. Her eyes flew to Lexi's to gauge how serious she was. Lexi had always been the more impulsive of the two of them and Willa, for the most part, has been okay with that. Although genetically they were identical, with the same blonde hair and blue eyes, Willa had never felt beautiful. She'd heard people joke that even between twins there was a prettier one, and that had always been Lexi.

It was something Willa accepted and Lexi reveled in. Lexi needed to be the center of attention. Even when they were little, Lexi had always wanted to be the first to hold something, the first to walk in line, the one people talked about the most after meeting them.

Willa, on the other hand, was naturally shy. She preferred people-watching instead of drawing attention to herself. She was cautious where Lexi was brash. In most cases it worked for them. Willa didn't need to be first at anything. She was happy to be her sister's biggest cheerleader.

But that wasn't how she felt with Lance.

Lexi must have seen the horror in her expression because she said, "I'm only kidding." Then she started toward the stairs. "You take everything so seriously. Come on. I'll race you to Lance."

Lexi took off down the stairs.

Willa tried to tell herself she didn't care, but she sprinted after Lexi. They came to a skidding stop in the hall when Kenzi's mother called out to them. "Girls!"

They turned toward her in unison.

Sophie Barrington was a delicately beautiful woman in her fifties. Her chestnut hair was gathered into a classical loose bun. The short-sleeved, collared, cotton dress she wore was tasteful and subdued. She looked exactly like what she was: a woman who had been born into wealth but had kept her life simple and focused on family.

Years ago, when Kenzi had first invited Willa and Lexi to visit her home, she'd briefly explained that her family had one unspoken rule no one, not even the eldest son, Asher, dared to break. Never ever upset Sophie. Willa had expected her to be a shrew, but the reality was Kenzi's mother had fallen apart after the loss of a child, and no one wanted to be the one to topple her a second time. It was hard not to feel sorry for the Barringtons. They were a huge family, but when given the chance they chose not to be together. They were all there that week for one reason—Sophie had asked them to come.

"How did you sleep last night? Do you have everything you need?" Sophie asked.

Willa answered enthusiastically, "It's beautiful, Mrs. Barrington. Thank you so much for letting us come."

Sophie smiled widely. "You know you girls are always welcome."

Lexi chimed in, "What's not to love? This place is like a hotel."

Sophie dismissed the twelve-bedroom, fourteen-bathroom beach mansion with a wave of her hand. "I don't like islands, but I used to enjoy the beach as a child—those were happy times. I told Asher we didn't need anything this big, but he likes to spoil us. I like to think we'll fill it with grandchildren one day and give the next generation the same happy memories." When neither Willa nor Lexi responded to that, Sophie bent and picked up a cloth bag from near the wall. "The boys are going out on jet skis. Could you be a dear and give this to Grant? There's a spray can of sunblock in there. Tell him to make sure they all wear some." She handed the bag to Willa. "You two should, too. It's easy to get a nasty burn."

Lexi made a face and Willa shook her head in subtle reprimand. Since their parents died in a plane crash when they were young, an older aunt and uncle had taken custody of the girls. It hadn't taken them long to deposit the girls at the boarding school. Being *mothered* by anyone felt unusual, but Lexi knew better than to buck it with Sophie. Willa rushed to assure Kenzi's mother they would definitely be careful.

With a satisfied smile, Sophie nodded at Willa. "I know you will, dear."

Lexi made a sound of displeasure deep in her throat but didn't say anything. Sophie never called either of them by name, and Lexi said it was because she couldn't tell them apart. Willa didn't want to believe it. Confusing them was the quickest way for the girls to lose their respect.

Lexi's smile turned impish. "We'll make sure your sons get sprayed all over."

Sophie's eyes rounded in surprise. Willa grabbed Lexi by the arm and pulled her toward the door. "We should run this down to them. See you later, Mrs. Barrington."

Lexi was still laughing when Willa closed the door to the house behind them. "Did you see her face?"

Willa shook her head in disapproval but couldn't help smiling. Lexi always was and probably always would be a ball-buster. "You're so bad."

Arm in arm with Willa, Lexi walked toward the dock. "You loved it."

Willa laughed. Part of Lexi's appeal was her in-your-face attitude. She didn't worry the way Willa did. "I hope she doesn't say anything to Kenzi about it."

Lexi shrugged. "If she does, I'll say *you* said it."

Willa gave her sister a playful hip check. "Do it. Kenzi would never believe it anyway."

Lexi's smile widened shamelessly. "You're probably right. Hey, on the bright side, we don't know how to drive a jet ski so that means we'll be cuddling up against some Barringtons today."

Willa smiled back but corrected, "Who see us as their little sister's friends."

Lexi arched an eyebrow at Willa and wrinkled her nose at Willa's T-shirt and shorts. "You, maybe, not me."

"Lexi—"

Her sister waved a hand in surrender. "Don't say it. I know. Really, Willa, you need to relax. There is nothing wrong with flirting. I'm not going to sleep with any of them. I'm not that stupid."

"THAT'S A LOT of beer," Lance said as his brother, Andrew, opened the large cooler from the back of the Jeep they'd used to drive supplies down to the beach.

"Want one?" Andrew cracked a can open and took a long gulp.

"I don't drink much," Lance said. Life was generally out of control enough without adding alcohol to it.

"You'd better not. You're not legal," Grant, the second oldest of the Barrington brothers, said sternly.

Andrew rolled his eyes. "The Marine Corp handed me an M16 at twenty, but the government won't let him have a beer? Give him a break."

In the same stern tone, Grant said, "I don't care if Lance has a few at college but not here. You shouldn't either."

Andrew took another deep gulp. "See, that makes me want to get shit-faced."

Asher walked over and lifted the top of the cooler. "Just beer?"

Lance gave his eldest brother a measured look. "Not up to your standards? Were you hoping for Macallan on the rocks? Money hasn't changed you at all, has it?"

Asher's expression tightened. "On your next birthday, you'll get the same amount I did. It's your choice if you want to do something with it or piss it away."

"Is that crack directed at me?" Andrew asked, straightening to his full height.

Asher didn't look at all bothered that he might have offended him. "No, you're throwing away your life, not your money. I look at you as an investment of sorts. If you're signing up for another two years, make sure your will is up to date."

Everyone was silent for a moment, then Grant said, "Not funny, Asher." He looked across at Andrew. "Andrew, keep your head down and don't get killed. But you should have a current will. That part was actually sound advice."

"Your concern is touching," Andrew said sarcastically.

Whatever Asher was about to say was interrupted by Ian's arrival. "It's a beautiful day. Let's not argue." He was well on his way to following in their father's political footsteps. When it suited him, he could be smooth and persuasive. But, he could also be a bull—and often was with the family. Lance figured that came from growing up so close in age with Grant and Asher. It was a case of step up or be stepped on. Although there was only a span of ten years between the oldest and youngest of them, their childhoods had been very different. Asher remembered life before their mother had her breakdown. He was old enough to have been affected by the scandal that had rocked the family. What he'd seen had hardened him. To some extent, Grant and Ian were the same. Lance, Andrew, and Kenzi on the other hand had been too young to understand. They only knew the aftermath. In some ways it had split the family in two: those who were angry and had become controlling asses, and those who had to put up with them.

Andrew faced the annoyance head-on. He held up his

drink. "Chill, Ian. It's all good." He threw a second beer to Lance, who caught it only because it would have hit him square in the chest if he hadn't. "Right, Lance?"

Lance survived his family by not engaging. Given a choice, he would have stayed at school during vacations, but that wasn't an option. When summoned home, they came. All of them, even the mighty Asher. Then, like puppets on strings, they would pretend to be close until they were given permission to leave again. It was pathetic, really, how little control even his very successful brothers had over this part of their lives. It should have made them less oppressive, but it hadn't.

It might have been the parental disapproving look his three oldest brothers were giving him or the fact that he and Andrew had always been close and he missed him, but Lance opened his beer and took a swig. "Absolutely."

Andrew looked past him and whistled. "Holy fuck, who is that?"

Lance turned and saw his sister's friends headed down the path toward the beach. He gave himself the luxury of appreciating the exposed expanse of Willa's long legs as the sound of her laughter carried across the distance to them. In the two years Kenzi had been bringing the twins around, they'd blossomed from giggling girls with braces to beautiful women—uncomfortably beautiful. "That's Willa and Lexi."

"No shit," Andrew said. "Wow. I should come home more often."

Grant made a disapproving sound. "Stand down. Those two are off limits. Kenzi considers them sisters. You should, too."

Andrew groaned. "That's not fair. How old are they?"

Asher went to stand beside Andrew. "Too young for you. They're eighteen."

Andrew made a face as he considered it. "Four years. Not that bad. But yeah, that's young. Damn, though. What a shame." He gave Lance a sideward look. "You, Lance, are the only one of us young enough. Lucky son of a bitch."

Lance opened his mouth to say that he would never see them as anything but Kenzi's friends but stopped when his eyes met Willa's. Despite the distance, his blood shot directly to his dick and his breath caught in his throat.

Ian clapped a hand on Lance's shoulder. "Not that lucky. Let's be really clear about something. None of us will ever get involved with any of Kenzi's friends, no matter who they are or how close they are to any of our ages. Things like that never end well."

Grant agreed. "It's already hard enough to get Kenzi to come home."

Looking unimpressed, Asher added, "If you're lonely, come see me when we get back to Boston. Trust me, there are plenty of women who look just like that who you can be with without the hassle."

Andrew gave Asher a skeptical look. "Twins? Who looks like that? I'd definitely be interested, but damn—"

Lance shook his head. He didn't care what Andrew thought of Lexi—but Willa. He didn't want anyone looking at her that way.

Andrew gave Lance a punch in the shoulder. "Don't try

to tell me it hasn't crossed your mind."

"They're not even that alike."

Andrew threw back his head and laughed. "Now I know you're fucking with me. They're creepy identical." When Lance didn't answer, Andrew gave him a curious look. "You can really tell them apart? How? Is it a mole or something?"

Lance watched the approaching twins and knew he'd never share his method. He'd confused them when they were younger, but since he'd seen them at their graduation a few months earlier he'd had no problem telling them apart. His body had a preference. When he looked at Lexi he saw a beautiful woman, but that was all. When he looked at Willa his whole body clenched like someone had punched him in the stomach and his dick throbbed painfully.

In the silence that followed Andrew's question, Grant said, "Willa dresses conservatively. So, Lexi's probably the one in the pink bikini."

Asher made an impatient sound. "Does it really matter which is which? Are we going out on the water, or not?"

Ian picked up the cooler and put it back on the jeep. "We're going."

Andrew threw his empty beer can down. "Yeah, this is getting old."

Willa and Lexi joined them. After shyly smiling at Lance, Willa walked over to Grant and handed him a cloth bag. "It's sunblock. Your mother is worried that you'll all burn."

Lexi winked. "If any of you need help putting it on . . ."

Three eldest male voices rang out in unison, "No." Grant passed an aerosol can around and each of them sprayed themselves down quickly before passing it to the next.

Lance didn't realize it was his turn until the can hit him in on the arm and dropped to the ground beside his feet. He bent to pick it up and sprayed himself absentmindedly. He couldn't look away from Willa. Hell, he could barely think. He reminded himself she was his sister's friend. Untouchable.

Willa smiled at him, and he struggled to not simply stand there, drooling. *Damn.* "Have you seen Kenzi?" she asked. Her perfectly pink lips were mesmerizing.

Grant answered, "Earlier. She said she'd be here. There are chairs and umbrellas set up if you want to wait for her over there."

"Oh," Willa said and then seemed embarrassed to have uttered that aloud. She blushed. "I mean, that's great."

Lance saw the disappointment in her eyes and swallowed hard. "Do you like to jet-ski?"

Her eyes were wide and innocent. "I don't know. I've never tried it."

Ian interceded, "Kenzi should be able to show you. She goes out alone."

Willa bit her bottom lip and hugged a towel to her stomach. "That'll be fine."

Lexi stepped forward. "Do you have enough for all of us? It can't be that hard. I'd try it by myself."

Asher walked away, clearly done with the conversation. Ian followed him. Before he left, Grant added in his irritating authoritative voice, "Only six. You can take turns with Kenzi."

After he'd gone, Lexi made a face. "So much for chivalry."

Willa hastened to smooth over her sister's comment. "It's fine, Lexi. We don't have to do it at all. This beach is gorgeous. I'll be happy just swimming and sunbathing."

Not able to help himself, Lance offered, "You could ride with me."

For a second excitement lit Willa's eyes, then she lowered her lashes shyly. "I don't want to take away from your fun."

Lance's mouth went dry and in a strangled voice he said, "You wouldn't. Come on."

Willa fell into step beside him then stopped. "Oh, my clothes." She stepped out of her flip-flops and whipped her T-shirt up and over her head. She folded it and placed it on her shoes then stepped out of her shorts.

Lance watched and wondered if he'd ever breathe again. *Kenzi's friend. Gorgeous, but still Kenzi's friend.*

Willa held out a hand toward him. "I probably need that."

For a wild moment Lance imagined her hand caressing his bare chest, teasing its way down his stomach and closing around his dick. *I need that, too.* He realized she was waiting for him to hand her something and shook the fantasy off. *Sunblock, idiot. She wants the sunblock.* He handed it to her. She closed her eyes and sprayed her face. Then she sprayed the length of her neck, down between two of the most perfect breasts he'd ever seen, along her beautiful arms. She was in a one-piece bathing suit, which should have been less sexy than the slips of cloth her sister was wearing, but it hugged every one of her curves perfectly. He was an internal wreck by the time she was done spraying the front of her long legs.

She held the can toward him. "Would you do my back?"

He nodded and took it. When she lifted her hair and exposed the curve of her neck to him, it took every shred of self-control he had not to lean down and kiss it. He applied the spray then tossed it. Possibly to Andrew, who he thought was talking to Lexi, but really he had no clue. He was trying to remember his own name. Willa effortlessly reduced him to that state.

Willa turned to thank him, and once again he almost stopped breathing. *Why did the one girl who turned his head have to be the one he couldn't have? Couldn't taste?* The expression in her beautiful blue eyes was warm, inviting, *trusting*. Her lips looked soft and so fucking kissable he ached. He was forced to look away before he made a fool of himself and kissed her right there in front of everyone.

Andrew winked at Lance, and the look he gave him said it all. Andrew would take Lexi out on the water to show their brothers they didn't control him. Lance doubted it would go further than that. Andrew might enjoy pissing off his brothers now and then, but he would never hurt anyone to do it.

Lance turned away. He would defy his brothers for a very different reason.

Willa smiled up at him with innocent desire in her eyes.

Right or wrong, he wanted her enough that nothing else mattered.

Chapter Two

Ten years later

WILLA CHAMBERS PUSHED a wayward blonde curl out of her eyes as she walked out of the Boston apartment she shared with Lexi. The warm August weather justified her white tank top and short jean skirt, but it was a more revealing outfit than she would have chosen for herself. She spoke nervously into the cell phone she was clutching near her ear. "I can't do this."

"It's too late to back out now," Lexi said.

"This isn't like the radio spot you had me do last week. No one will believe I'm you."

"People won't have a reason to question who you are unless you give them one."

"I could never dance as well as you."

"Only because you held yourself back. You've got this, Willa. Besides, it's not like we won't get paid even if you mess up. You know Clay Landon. He's a friend of Dax."

"Which is another reason I feel weird about saying I'm you."

"Stop. No one cares if it's really me or not. Clay asked

me to create an experience for his friend. That's what we're giving him. The dance company I hired is amazing. This isn't their first flash mob. You rehearsed the moves with me. The rest is easy."

"You should have canceled."

"No, I should have taken the day out of this temp job to be there. Dancing for the suits in the financial district sounds a hundred times more fun than what I'm doing today."

Willa heard a hint of discontent in her sister's voice and was instantly worried. "I thought you said you liked working at Poly-Shyn."

Lexi sighed. "I'm not quitting it, if that's what you're afraid of. It pays the rent, and one of us needs a steady income."

Low blow, but after all the times I've spoken to her about the importance of sticking to one job, I guess I deserved it. I certainly didn't imagine my future consisting of unemployment and taking gigs Lexi sends my way. Willa thought back to the art cataloging job she'd taken for an auction house. She'd thought it was secure when she and Lexi had relocated to Boston to be near Kenzi. Willa's life had been right on track, and then, wham, they'd let her go. After ten months of looking for something in the art world, Willa was getting desperate. She was used to being the responsible sister, but somehow that had all gone to shit since moving to the United States. "I'm sorry, I'll find a permanent job soon."

"Don't be sorry, Willa, be spectacular today. Even after we pay the dance company, you'll make enough to pay off some of the debt we've accumulated. Which we wouldn't have, by the way, if you'd taken the job Kenzi's fiancée offered you at his company."

"I didn't go to college so I could be a glorified typist."

"Like me."

Willa wiped away a bead of sweat from the back of her neck. She wasn't trying to diminish what her sister was doing. In fact, she was impressed Lexi had stayed as long as she had. Lexi was notorious for going through jobs as quickly as she went through men. It was only recently that she'd become serious about earning a steady income. Willa also wasn't used to arguing with her sister, at least never about anything serious. Not since—well, not in a very long time. *None of this is worth fighting over.* "I'm proud of you, Lexi. Ignore my mood. I've never been comfortable being the center of attention. You know that. What if I trample the person next to me and embarrass you?"

Lexi made a supportive sound. "You'll be fine. Stop thinking about everything that could go wrong, and let yourself enjoy today. Clay said he wanted to make his friend laugh. Above everything else, it's supposed to be fun."

Fun. Willa laughed nervously and flagged down a cab. She gave the driver the address Lexi had given her. *Life isn't about having fun. It's a game of survival. Hold on the best you can because it can be one hell of a rough ride.*

She would have said that aloud, but Lexi would never understand. How they could be so alike physically and have such different personalities never ceased to amaze Willa. She knew Lexi felt the same. Her sister made it her mission to push Willa into situations she thought would help her "break out of her shell." The problem was, Willa didn't want to break out. She'd tried to be like Lexi once and had learned her lesson. Never again.

Except today, but this is different. It's just a job. Willa groaned as she tugged at the hem of the skirt Lexi had left out for her to wear. She looked at the high heels that were a good two inches higher than she normally would have worn. "I hope I don't fall flat on my face."

"If you do, the video will definitely go viral."

"Video?" Willa's stomach did a nervous flip. "I'm serious. I have a bad feeling about today."

With an impatient sound, Lexi said, "God. Should I say I'm sick and cut out of here?"

Willa gave herself a mental slap. Lexi was finally doing well. *I need to do this—for both of us.* "No. You're right. I practiced the moves with you. I'll be fine."

"Yes, you will be. Remember, everyone will already be there, and they'll know what to do. I told them what you're wearing so even those who've never met me will recognize you. All you have to do is go up to whoever Clay is standing with and congratulate him."

"Who am I congratulating and for what?"

"Clay didn't say, but does it matter? As soon as you speak, the crowd will freeze. The first few dancers will come out and circle around you. Don't move until the music starts. We have about eighty-five people scheduled to join in different waves until you're all dancing together."

"And I'm in front the whole time?"

"I would be."

If this doesn't make my ass willing to take whatever next job I'm offered, nothing will. "Okay."

"When the song ends everyone will stop dancing and return to doing whatever they were before, as if nothing happened. You can leave then. That's it. It's the easiest five grand you'll ever make."

The taxi stopped at a light, and Willa felt foolish for making such a big deal out of it. Lexi had walked her through the choreography and the moves. It would be easy enough to fall into step with those around her. Clay's client wouldn't know if she took a wrong step as long as she flowed with them. *I can do this.* "I appreciate the work you put into this, Lexi. I may not sound grateful, but I am."

"I know, Willa. And, seriously, I would have canceled if I didn't think you could do this."

"You're making dinner tonight."

"I can't. I'm working late. But I'll do the grocery shopping this week. How's that?"

"Deal," Willa said. The taxi pulled up to a spot outside a tall glass building that had a grass courtyard, an unusual luxury in an otherwise stale background of buildings. Willa paid the driver then did her best to get out of the car gracefully, not an easy feat, considering her outfit. She studied the people in the area. Outside of the number of people gathered, there was no hint they didn't belong there. Anyone walking by would have thought a conference or meeting had just released its participants for lunch. Their professional attire made Willa feel even more out of place. If the dancers were already there, they blended in well. *Unlike me.*

Willa felt the gaze of several men follow her as she approached the building. She was used to a certain amount of male attention, but she felt exposed. *How does Lexi live like this?* As she walked toward the building, she wished Lexi were there to draw the attention away from her.

She caught her shoulders hunching forward in response to her natural shyness and forced herself to straighten them. *I'm Lexi—at least for the next fifteen minutes.*

There was no sign of Clay, and for a moment Willa worried she might have given the driver the wrong address. She was getting ready to ask the woman closest to her if she knew Clay Landon when a black sedan pulled up in front of the building. She'd met him a couple of times through Kenzi but only briefly. The more nervous she became the less she could remember what he looked like. A tall blond man stepped out of a limo and looked around. He was attractive in a European chic kind of way. Although he was dressed in jeans and a collared shirt, he had an aura of someone at the top of the one percent. He smiled when he saw her and nodded.

Willa wobbled on her high heels when she recognized the man who got out of the car next. *No. No. No.*

He's Clay's friend? Surely Lexi hadn't known who would be here.

There was only one man Willa would not dance for, one man who had hurt her deeply enough that she'd protected her heart ever since.

Lance Barrington.

Willa took a step back and the movement caught Lance's attention. He cocked his head to one side and raised a hand in greeting to her. Willa retreated another step. Clay urged Lance forward.

"You're going the wrong way," a man whispered to her. The way he said it made Willa certain he was with the dance company.

Willa didn't care. Her impromptu plan was to get as far away from there as quickly as she could. "No, I'm not."

There was a buzz of hushed talking around her until she backed into a woman who didn't move. She smiled at Willa as if she were apologizing for being in her way, but her voice was a cold challenge. "What are you doing?"

"I'm leaving," Willa said honestly, apologetically.

The woman's eyes narrowed. "I didn't hire a cameraman so you could flake out at the last minute. You're the cue for us to start. You can either walk over there as planned or pay the videographer yourself. Your choice. My dancers will also need to be compensated. We signed a contract."

Willa swallowed hard. She barely had the rent money for next month. She couldn't pay anyone's salary. She looked back at Lance and mild panic set in. Both he and Clay were walking toward her.

Next to Clay, Lance looked rough around the edges. Two athletic builds, but Lance was the rugby player and Clay more of the golf type. Why couldn't Lance have gotten a potbelly and gone bald with time? Why did he have to get better looking every time Willa saw him? Just as it had when she was younger, her body warmed with a craving only he could feed.

Why does just looking at him excite me more than any other man's touch ever has?

He came to a stop in front of her, a puzzled look of concern on his face. "Willa?"

His question flamed an old anger within her, and on impulse she said, "Lexi."

He frowned.

Willa told herself to let the past go, but she was shaking from the emotional charge of old memories. *Why can't I put it behind me? Because he's always there, part of my life even if I wish he weren't.*

Lexi knew better than to mention his name. Willa loved her sister, but even as close as they were, they'd both done things to hurt each other—things they regretted, things apologies didn't fully wash away. Lance was a reminder of a time Willa never wanted to relive. She didn't feel bad about telling him she was Lexi. He didn't deserve the truth. The quicker she started this fiasco, the quicker she could leave. "Congratulations."

With large, dramatic moves, an assortment of male and female dancers tore off their suits, revealing casual street clothing. Clay stepped away. The dancers encircled Lance and Willa. The opening music to a song began to play loudly.

The scene felt unreal. Lance looked around in surprise then back at her. The words from the song had meant nothing to Willa when she'd practiced the dance moves to them with Lexi, but suddenly, hearing them while so close to Lance threw Willa off balance.

What would I give for one taste of your lips?

One night in your arms?
I'd trade it all.

The song seemed to affect Lance as well. There was a fire in his eyes, hinting at a need that mirrored her own.

For Lexi.

To him, we're the same.

Inhibitions temporarily pushed aside, Willa waved her arms, matching the movements of the dancers behind her. She threw herself into the energy and the power of the crowd. As more and more people came forward, stripped off their business attire and began to dance in T-shirts and cut-off jeans, Willa shifted away from Lance to move in unison with them. They formed a large semicircle that covered the lawn and flowed out onto the sidewalk behind.

The words of the song fanned Willa's confusion.

You looked right through me, walked right by.
But you see me now.
Come on, give me one taste, one night.
We'll do it all.

She let the music flow through her, drive her movements. Her eyes held Lance's even though they were twenty or so feet from each other.

I may have been easy enough to forget before. She glanced at him over her shoulder and deliberately wiggled her ass at him. *But try to forget this.*

WHAT HAD STARTED as an interesting and productive day had derailed into a spectacle Lance was struggling to make sense of. If his cock's judgment could be trusted, there was no way in hell the woman who had just congratulated him was Lexi Chambers. He'd found many women attractive in his near thirty years, Lexi being one of them, but only one woman had the irritating ability to give him a public boner.

Willa Chambers.

The flash mob organized into four lines of dancers with Willa in the front. The overall scene might have been impressive but, like a schoolboy, Lance's attention was drawn to the bounce of two perfectly rounded breasts. His gaze lingered on Willa's deliciously long, bare legs before she spun, and he was treated to the equally tantalizing view of her perfect little ass beneath a skirt that barely covered it. She shook that delightful derriere back and forth with a seductive rhythm, until all he wanted to do was reach out and haul it against his throbbing cock. Lance gritted his teeth and forced himself to look away. There were many women dancing, several with more provocative outfits than Willa's, but they couldn't hold his attention. Every move Willa made, every time their gazes met and clashed, Lance's blood pounded in a possessive, primal way.

That has to be Willa.

His body knew hers, remembered every intimate, delectable inch of her. There was no way to block the memories of her tongue eagerly meeting his. How was it possible that none of the women he'd been with over the past ten years had shaken him to the core as she had? Yes, she was gorgeous, but why Willa? He didn't regret much in his life, but if he could go back in time he would have stayed away from her that week.

Or been with her every week since.

His only excuse was he'd been young with a disproportionate ratio of more hormones than brains. He'd considered himself intelligent, but with her he'd been a bumbling fool—making mistake after mistake until he'd ruined any chance they'd had of being together.

Proof of the level of his screwup was the length of time Willa had held a grudge. She was civil to him in social situations, but that was all. At first, he'd tried to make amends. She'd said she never wanted to see him again, and he'd wanted to understand why. Eventually, out of respect for her friendship with his sister, he'd backed off. Time should have smoothed things over between them, but it hadn't. One night. It shouldn't still be that big of a deal, but it was. He'd given up hope that she'd ever forgive him. His cock, on the other hand, had remained more optimistic.

Normally, Willa made every effort to avoid Lance. *So why is she dancing for me? And why pretend she's Lexi?*

"Congratulations on getting the Capitol Complex," Clay said and gave his shoulder a clap of approval.

Lance shook his head to clear it. "That's what this is about?" He yanked his attention away from Willa long enough to assess Clay's expression. "What if I hadn't closed the deal today?"

Clay smiled smoothly. "My plan B was to have her say, 'Better luck next time.' Either way, it's quite a show; am I right?"

"You have too much time on your hands." Lance turned his attention back to Willa. *I know what I'd like on my hands. On my anything.* Lance groaned. *Stop. This is how I fucked it up the first time.*

"Having fun?"

No. This is torture, that's what it is, Lance thought but didn't say.

"Your sister has beautiful taste in friends. Twins. Seriously. And you've known them since high school? Tell me you've had them both, preferably together. No, don't tell, it'll ruin my fantasy of doing the same."

The idea of Clay with Willa sliced through Lance. He snarled, "Shut the fuck up."

Clay raised his hands in mock fear. "Not even willing to share one? I'll take either. Honestly, I can't tell them apart."

"Then you're blind. That's Willa."

Clay's eyebrows shot up. He turned his head to watch Willa as she was picked up and twirled around by a male dancer. "Not Lexi? Do they pretend to be each other often? That's hot."

"No, it's not," Lance said unhappily. *We've known each other for twelve years. Does she think I would ever confuse them now?*

Clay rubbed his chin and looked Lance over again. "Just ask her out."

With a frown, Lance leaned in aggressively. "Drop it." He hadn't known what to think of Clay when Dax and Kenzi had first brought him around. Lance didn't have much respect for the typical super-rich silver spoons, who had been handed their fortunes. They were often weak, vain, and in search of entertainment regardless of how it affected others. He, on the other hand, had been brought up with a strong work ethic and knew what a day's work meant. He was no silver-spooner.

Lance was an architect. His buildings were designed to stand the test of time and weather. Extremely utilitarian. He and his brothers had worked hard to achieve what they had. Yes, they'd been given large trust funds, but only after they'd already established themselves. They didn't have time to be bored or plan fucking flash mobs.

Dax had warned Lance that Clay had been born with more money than God and would go to extreme lengths to avoid boredom. *Which explains gyrating dancers instead of a card.*

Dax had joked that Clay looked lonely since he'd been spending so much time with Kenzi. He'd asked Lance to include him in on a project. Clay not only wouldn't expect compensation, he would bring his network of connections to any endeavor.

But this—this is him fucking with me.
He's testing how I feel about her.

Yes, Clay had real estate expertise for the city project Lance had bid on, but he had yet to share any of it. Clay's appreciation for historical buildings and his reputation for optimizing the value of a property was the main reason Lance had agreed. However, the price of working with Clay was proving higher than it was worth.

He asked personal questions a Barrington would never ask, never mind answer. His general level of interest in all things Barrington had been one reason Lance had agreed to entertain him. He'd wanted to shift Clay's attention to something besides the inner workings of his family. It had worked.

And now, it had backfired.

Clay looked amused. "So angry. Why? You shouldn't want to punch me for having the woman you're lusting over dance in that skimpy outfit, you should thank me. I don't even have feelings for her, and it's turning me on."

Lance raised a hand to grab the front of Clay's shirt as a rush of anger surged through him. It was only the pleased expression on the other man's face that held him in check. Clay was trying to get a rise out of him, and it was working. Lance took a deep breath and rubbed a hand over the back of his neck in frustration. "You need to back the fuck off."

"Maybe," Clay said with a chuckle.

"What the hell is your problem?" Lance growled. *No amount of expert advice is worth this shit.* Lance turned away from Clay and realized the music had ended, the dancers had dispersed, and Willa was gone. He swore beneath his breath.

"What would stop you from hooking up with her?" Clay gave Lance a long measured look. "She was upset when she saw you. You have history, don't you?"

"No," Lance lied. What he'd shared with Willa was none of Clay's business. "Stop looking for something where there is nothing."

"Good, I could have a go at someone like that."

This time Lance couldn't control his response. He grabbed the front of Clay's shirt with one hand while fisting his other. "If you go anywhere near Willa—"

Clay pushed his hand off him and straightened his shirt.

"Don't wrinkle the Hugo Boss."

Lance ran a hand through his hair, striving to regain control of himself. Some of his brothers were known for their short tempers, but he'd always been the more levelheaded one. He was also a strategist. To win against Mother Nature, an architect needed to imagine worst-case scenarios and plan accordingly. Neither anger nor love had ever made a building stronger. Careful, educated decisions executed with solid, quality materials always produced reliable results. It was how Lance designed buildings and how he lived his life.

He didn't brawl with friends of the family. That was Asher's style, not his.

Which didn't change how much he wanted to punch the smug smile off Clay's face. *I don't need this. Dax will have to find a new source of entertainment for his friend.* "I've changed my mind about using you as a consultant on this project." He looked around the grassy area in disgust. "Next time you want to congratulate someone—send a fucking fruit basket." He turned and walked away.

Chapter Three

RATHER THAN HAILING a cab, Willa strode down the busy sidewalk, indifferent to her feet protesting the wrong shoes for a prolonged stomping away. She yanked her phone out of the pocket of her jean skirt and glared at a man whose eyebrows rose appreciatively as the act lifted one side of her skirt. She was so angry she wanted to scream, and her expression must have communicated that because the man quickly looked away. Without breaking her pace, Willa called Lexi. It rang through to her voice messages.

Did Lexi know? Had Clay told her?
I want to believe he didn't.
She didn't.
But I know Lexi.

Willa called right back. This time her sister answered.

"You knew." Willa ground out, not wasting time greeting her sister.

"Knew what?" Lexi answered innocently. Too innocently.

While waiting for a light to change, Willa continued, not caring that the people near could hear. "That Lance was the person the flash mob was for. You humiliated me."

Lexi's silence was all the confession Willa required.

Willa crossed the street with the crowd when the light changed and waited for her sister to say something, anything that would make what she'd done okay.

In a subdued voice, Lexi said, "That wasn't my intention."

So, I was right. Where do we go from here? "It's never your intention, but that doesn't change the outcome. I am so angry with you. I don't want to go back to our apartment. I can't afford to go anywhere else, but that's going to change. I think it's time for you and me to get our own places."

"You're not serious. I thought—"

"No. You didn't. You didn't think about how I would feel, or you wouldn't have done this to me."

"So, what? You move out, hate me forever, and we'll never talk again? Calm down, Willa; it's not that big of a deal."

"To you. It's not that big of a deal *to you.*" Stopping at another street crossing, Willa brushed her hair impatiently out of her eyes and said, "Nothing ever is. I love you, but I remember this feeling. We've been here before. I don't want to go back to thinking I can't trust you. We're almost thirty. Maybe it's not healthy for us to live together anymore."

"If you think we're broke now, wait until each of us is paying our own rent."

"I don't care. I'll make it work."

"You wouldn't be happy living on your own. You need more people in your life, not fewer."

"Don't tell me what I need."

"Really? You can say that after recently passing judgment on every aspect of my life?"

The anger in Lexi's tone struck a chord in Willa and deflated some of hers. "I only said what you needed to hear."

"In your opinion," Lexi said shortly. "You dismissed everything I've done because I deviated from *your* rule book. Do you know how it felt to hear how little you respect my choices?"

Willa paused mid-step. "So, you wanted to prove I'm more messed up than you? Is that why you set today up? Because you wanted to win?"

"No. Willa, how could you even ask that?" Lexi sounded more offended than apologetic.

Despite the people passing her on both sides, Willa covered her face with one hand. She remembered accusing Lexi of something similar when they'd argued over Lance many years earlier. They truly had come full circle, back to a dark place. Someone bumped into Willa and brought her back to the moment, making her aware of how public her emotional display was. "Let's talk about this tonight."

"Let's not. I really don't want to go twenty rounds with you about something you've already made your mind up about. I'm working late then going out. Don't wait up for me tonight."

Regardless of how upset she was with her sister, Willa loved Lexi. She struggled to verbalize how she was feeling. Her greatest fear was losing her sister. Her second greatest was losing herself in Lexi's shadow. "Lexi, I don't want to fight with you either, but this was wrong."

"Fine, I was wrong. Keep hiding from the world, but don't blame me when that stops you from having the life you want. If you want to move out, Willa, move out. Or I will. Maybe you need to see what it's like to not have me looking out for you. Maybe that's what it'll take for you to appreciate me." Lexi hung up.

Appreciate her? How can she think I don't appreciate her? She's my best friend. My twin. Of course I appreciate her. I chose being with her over everything else. Everyone else.

Willa pocketed her phone and hailed a taxi. Her anger had dissolved, and in its place was a feeling of emptiness she didn't know what to do with. She'd put the past behind her. Nothing but pain would come from looking back.

On the ride back to her apartment, she considered calling Kenzi but didn't. When it came to this situation, there was too much Kenzi didn't know, would never know.

Willa entered her apartment and placed her phone and keys on the tray she'd purchased to keep the entryway organized. Lexi had probably placed her keys in the tray twice in all the time they'd lived together, and likely only by mistake. She was much more the type to walk in, toss her keys in the general direction of the table, and keep going. Willa had always gone back and put them where they belonged. She didn't see how Lexi thought she was the one who needed taking care of.

Unless she knows.

But there is no way she could.

On the way to her bedroom, Willa stopped when she

caught her reflection in a mirror across the room. Dressed as she was, at first glance, she could be Lexi.

Did Lance believe me when I said I was Lexi?
Does it matter? After all this time, it shouldn't.
And I shouldn't be this angry.

Lexi isn't a bad person. She just doesn't think things through. The ripple effect of her impulsiveness was lost on her. Like a person who runs across the street without looking and wonders why two cars crashed behind her, Lexi was blind to the devastation she sometimes wreaked. How much was a person's fault and how much would have happened anyway? It was a question Lexi and Willa never agreed on.

Willa changed into yoga pants and a T-shirt. She took out her laptop and sat on the couch. Whether she stayed or moved out, she needed a job. She started to write an email to Dax, asking if he still had a position for her, but then decided to call him later instead.

She didn't feel ready to speak to him or Kenzi yet, not after seeing Lance that morning. *I should have told him it was me. I should have acted like seeing him was no big deal.*

Instead, I hid behind a lie.

I'm a coward. No wonder he chose her.

Willa forced herself off the couch and headed to the gym, taking her reader tablet with her. She ran on a treadmill much longer that day than she normally would have, both because the story she'd chosen was a good one and because she didn't want to rush back to her life.

She ran until she was too tired to care what Lance thought of her.

Too tired to worry where Lexi was headed that night.

She ran until she was dripping with sweat and her muscles were shaking from the exertion. Only then did she stop. Another woman might have released the tension of the day by crying, but Willa never allowed herself that luxury.

Crying had never solved a problem. It hadn't brought her parents back.

Wishing things were different was a waste of time.

I have to find a job—and now.

When I do, I won't have time to argue with Lexi or waste another moment thinking about a man I should have purged from my system a decade ago.

THE NEXT DAY Lance was seated at the dining room table with his parents and all of his siblings except Andrew. Dax looked comfortable in his spot beside Kenzi. A visibly pregnant Emily was seated beside Asher. There was an air of anticipation that had made the meal drag a bit, but no one was asking why they'd been summoned that evening. If the expression on his mother's face was a clue, it wasn't bad news.

Sophie took her husband's hand in hers. "Our family has had quite a year." She smiled at Emily then Dax. "But we're better for the changes as well as the additions."

Emily used her napkin to wipe a tear away from her eyes. Dax merely nodded, but Lance could tell her words had pleased him.

Dale added, "Asher and Emily have an announcement."

Lance joked, "She's pregnant."

Emily laid a hand on her very round stomach. "It shows?" Emily asked with a laugh.

Lance watched Asher smile simply because Emily had and envied his brother for a moment. He'd never wanted to follow in his brother's footsteps. In fact, there had been a time when he'd wondered if he had enough in common with Asher to bother to see him more often than at the holidays and during the one week each year when his family gathered to mourn the loss of Kenzi's twin. That feeling had changed since Asher had gotten engaged. Emily had brought out a softer side of his brother, as well as dragged his family together twice a month for what she called game nights. At first everyone had attended them simply because doing so had made their mother happy. Over time, though, it seemed to bring them closer. Emily had done that, as well as brought life to Asher's eyes that hadn't been there before.

Lance didn't put much faith in the idea of love, but he could tell his brother did. It was the ability to believe that any of this would last that Lance envied. In concept love was a beautiful thing, but in reality it was fragile and short-lived. Nothing an intelligent man invested too much of his time or energy into. Most relationships fell to pieces in less than a year.

He hoped Asher and Emily were the exception.

Asher put his arm around Emily. "Emily and I have been dragging our feet regarding the location for our wedding."

"As long as it happens before the baby arrives," Dale said.

Sophie clasped her hands together. "I've offered to help you."

Glancing up at Asher, Emily added, "And we appreciate that, but weddings are really stressful. We had my museum opening and the groundbreaking on the school in New Hampshire." She rubbed her baby bump. "Plus this little one. I'm exhausted."

Asher kissed Emily on the temple then said, "We hope you'll understand when we say we eloped. Emily and I are married. We had a small, private ceremony the last time we were in New Hampshire, and we'd like to consider tonight our wedding reception."

Collectively there was a hesitation as everyone waited for how Sophie would handle the news. Even though her children were all adults, *her* mood and reaction still set the tone for everyone around her. Kenzi had recently shaken the family up by breaking her silence about something she'd held in out of deference to their mother. Lance was proud of her for finding her voice. It was ironic that the youngest of them had become the boldest.

Braver than the rest of us.

Sophie covered her cheeks with both hands and rose to her feet. "I would have loved to see the ceremony, Emily, but I'm so happy I can finally, officially, call you my daughter."

Emily stood and the two exchanged an emotional embrace.

Lance met Grant's relieved gaze from across the table. They were both thinking the same thing: *That could have gone either way.*

Ian was the first to walk over and congratulate Asher. Their father was sporting a huge smile when he walked over to hug Emily and then Asher.

Even Dax, someone Lance had initially struggled imagining as part of the family, shook Asher's hand and seemed genuinely happy for him. Kenzi was out of her seat, bubbling over in excitement.

Grant rose to his feet to congratulate the happy couple and Lance followed. He pushed aside the way his brother's happiness made him feel about his own life and clapped Asher on the back then hugged Emily. "One sister was rough. What will I do with two?"

In response to being called his sister, Emily burst into tears. "I'm sorry I'm bawling, but I am so grateful to be part of this family. You have no idea how much all of you mean to me."

Asher hugged his new wife to his side and kissed the top of her head. "You mean every bit as much to all of us."

Dale looked around at his children and nodded in approval. "You do, Emily. You've been a real gift to this family."

Sophie slid beneath her husband's arm and hugged him. She smiled up at him. "One of our babies is married."

Asher shook his head and Emily wagged a finger at him. Asher arched an eyebrow in challenge, and she blushed. Lance looked away when the couple's expressions revealed they were having a very intimate, albeit wordless, conversation.

Dale nodded at Kenzi. "Now you, young lady, will break my heart if you rob me of the opportunity to walk you down the aisle."

Kenzi glanced up at Dax then at her father. "Don't worry, Dad, I want a big wedding. Huge. Dax and I have already started planning it. It'll be down in Clearwater, Florida, on one of Clay Landon's properties. I can't wait to show you the place."

Emily looked down at her stomach again. "Are you sure you still want me in your wedding party?"

Kenzi nodded vigorously. "We can wait until after the baby is here. I don't mind. I'm thinking that a beach wedding in late spring would be beautiful." She glanced at her fiancé. "Dax?"

"If we leave married I'll be happy with whatever, wherever, and whenever."

Her level of confidence in something Lance didn't believe in made him uncomfortable enough that he excused himself from the conversation. He strode out of the house onto the steps that led to the driveway. He'd never smoked, but he wished for a moment that he did. It would have given him a reason to need to step outside. He sat on the top step and hung his hands between his knees, neither analyzing his feelings nor successfully shaking them off enough to go back inside.

A few minutes later, the door behind him opened. "Mind if I join you?" Without waiting for permission, Kenzi sat down on the step beside Lance. "Are you okay?"

Lance knocked his shoulder against his sister's then continued to stare out over the cars lined up in the driveway. "I'm fine. I just needed some air."

Kenzi shoved her shoulder against his and said, "If I've

learned anything from being with Dax, it's that honesty, however uncomfortable it may make a situation at first, is always better. Tell me whatever is bothering you is none of my business, but don't lie to me and say you're fine."

Lance let out an impatient sigh and ran a hand through his hair. "I'm not lying. There's nothing wrong."

In a quiet voice, Kenzi said, "I don't believe you."

Lance ruffled his sister's hair as he had when they were much younger. "So serious. Stop looking for issues where there are none. It was getting stuffy inside."

"I can see how you'd want to come out here and cool off in this ninety-degree weather. I'm melting."

Lance stood and offered his sister his hand. "Me, too."

Kenzi took his hand and held on to it even once she was standing. "I love you, Lance, and how you feel matters to me. When you do want someone to talk to, remember I'm here for you. Always."

Lance gave Kenzi a quick hug. "Come on, squirt. Let's go in."

Just before they opened the door, Kenzi said, "Clay came over for dinner last night."

Lance tensed. "And?"

"He said the two of you had had a falling out."

"More of a difference of opinion."

"He implied he wouldn't be working with you on the Capitol Complex."

"That's right."

"What happened?"

Lance opened the door of the house and held it while

Kenzi walked through. "It was a miscalculation on my part to involve him in the project. He's flashy where I'm practical. Our visions for the complex wouldn't have melded well."

Once inside the house, Kenzi turned and blocked Lance's entry. "It sounded like more than the complex."

Lance closed the door impatiently behind him and stepped around Kenzi. "Drop it, Kenzi. I don't want to talk about it." He started walking away.

Kenzi put a hand on one hip. "Willa called last night while Clay was there."

Lance stopped but didn't say anything.

"She asked Dax if he still had a job for her. I thought you should know that Clay jumped in and said he has a position that would be perfect for her."

I bet he does. Lance's temper rose, and his hands fisted at his sides. He slowly turned on his heel back to face his sister. "Did she take it?"

"She hasn't decided, but she's going for an interview with him tomorrow."

"What is she thinking? He has a handful of employees, but no company. As far as I know he flits around the globe, choosing his projects on whims."

"However he does it, he's successful at it. Travel was something he highlighted as a perk of working for him. Willa hasn't been many places. He said he'd love to change that."

I'll kill him. Lance realized he'd made a growling sound deep in his throat when both of his sister's eyebrows flew up.

With rounded, innocent eyes, Kenzi added, "Willa has

always had an artistic eye. Someone like that might be useful on your project."

Surprised, Lance asked, "She's interested in working for me?"

Kenzi rolled her eyes. "Not that she has said, but you could offer her something and see."

Lance imagined how little he'd be able to concentrate on anything but her if she worked in his building. He had a policy prohibiting office affairs. They were a distraction, just as she would be. "I can't hire Willa."

Kenzi shrugged and linked arms with Lance and urged him to walk back to the dining room with her. "I imagine she'll take the job with Clay, then."

Lance ground his teeth together but kept his thoughts to himself. *Like hell she will.* He rejoined his family just long enough to appease them before making a hasty exit.

He wasn't about to sit back and let Clay manipulate Willa for amusement. He remembered every comment Clay had made about being with one or both of them simply because they were twins. Lance didn't know how much of what Clay had said had been real and how much had been bullshit he'd thrown out to see what would get a rise out of him, but Lance wasn't taking any chances.

As he pulled out of the driveway, he gave into an impulse he'd fought against but lost. Although he never used it, he had Willa's number in his contacts. He said, "Call Willa."

Her line rang two, three, four times before going to voicemail.

"Hi, you've reached Willa Chambers. Sorry I missed you.

Leave a message."

Beep.

"Willa, it's Lance. Call me when you get this." He considered saying more, but hung up instead. It was probably a good thing she hadn't answered. He was still trying to figure out what to say to her.

Chapter Four

➤➤➤❰❰❰

IN AN OVERSIZED T-shirt and shorts, Willa was seated on the couch in her living room with her laptop and a cup of coffee. She'd spent the last hour writing and editing her résumé to hand to Clay when she interviewed with him the next day. Although the job had come to her because he was a friend of a friend, Willa wanted to show him she would take it seriously.

The problem was he hadn't exactly given many details about the job description. He'd said he needed a traveling assistant. That had to require organizational skills. *I'm a natural organizer.* Willa listed her past jobs that would document her ability to do just that. So much of what she'd done in the past had been solitary work. She didn't know how she'd do being with someone as gregarious as Clay, but she told herself she could handle whatever life threw at her.

Haven't I already proven that?

She read as much as she could about the duties of an assistant then crafted her résumé in a way she hoped would make her sound qualified.

When Dax had first put Clay on the phone with her,

Willa had felt awkward, but it was quickly apparent that Clay saw her only as Lexi's quiet sister. He didn't seem to have any idea that it had been her dancing in the flash mob. Then he'd offered her a salary that would allow her to make in a couple months what she was used to making in a year. With that job, she could put money aside. No, it wasn't in her field or something she was passionate about, but Lexi was right about one thing: *the bank doesn't care how much I do or don't like where I work. It's time for me to stop thinking about what I want to do and focus on what I have to do. I have to pay my bills, and this will allow me to do that.* With that mindset, she'd put aside her concerns about not being qualified and decided she would not only get that job, but also excel at it.

Her phone rang. *Lance Barrington.*

It went through to voicemail while she was still debating with herself if she should answer him. After she played his message back, she hurriedly closed her laptop and stood. She played the message back again.

If Lance weren't Kenzi's brother, Willa would have played the message to her. If Willa had talked to Lexi since their argument, she would have called her and done the same.

Lance didn't call her. Not anymore. Not since she'd told him to never call her again.

Willa played the message once more. He didn't sound happy.

Did he find out it was me at the flash mob? Is he upset that I lied to him?

Upset I wasn't Lexi?

I won't know if I don't call him.
Sometimes not knowing is better.
Stop.

Willa called Lance back and held her breath. *I'm not eighteen anymore. I can handle the truth now.* "Hi Lance. You called?"

"Are you home?"

Willa glanced down at what was technically her pajamas then at the clock. It was seven o'clock on a Thursday night. *No wonder Lexi thinks I don't have a life.* "Yes. What do you need?"

"I'm on my way over."

Willa dropped the phone then scrambled to pick it back up. "Sorry about that. Slippery phone case. Did you say you're on your way here?"

"I did."

"Lexi's at work."

"That's fine. It's you I have to talk to."

Have to? Shit. Don't panic. It's probably nothing. "About anything in particular?"

"I'd rather talk about it when I'm there."

Willa glanced down at herself again. Her heart was thudding wildly in her chest. "I'm actually busy tonight. I'm finishing up something I need done for tomorrow. Can this wait?"

Like until never?

"What are you working on? Anything I could help you with?"

She would have loved to have been able to respond with

something impressive. The truth was almost too lame to voice aloud. *I'm almost thirty and*—"I'm tweaking my résumé."

"I hire people all the time. I could give you some suggestions."

I'm sure you could, but I can't be alone with you. It hurts too much. Willa imagined how the evening would go if she said yes to him coming over. She'd rush around like a maniac throwing on clothing she hoped made her look good. She'd do her makeup like a madwoman. By the time he'd arrive she'd be in a nervous sweat and hating herself for it. *For nothing. No.* "Sorry, Lance, but tonight's not good. I don't want company. I do have a minute, though, if you need to ask me something."

"I just pulled up to the front of your building."

Panic set in. *Sorry, I've already met my quota when it comes to making a fool of myself over you.* "You're not hearing what I'm saying, Lance."

"And that is?"

Willa closed her eyes and bit her bottom lip before answering. *This isn't supposed to be hard. He's not supposed to matter anymore.* "I don't want to see anyone tonight. Goodnight. Sorry you drove over here for nothing."

Willa hung up and glared at her reflection across the room. She was a tangle of resentment. She'd closed the door on that time in her life and nothing good could come from opening it. *I shouldn't have called him back.* Hearing his voice . . . hearing the way he said her name . . . *Why can't I leave that door shut? I have to get this job with Clay, anything to get me away from Boston even if only for a short time. Just long enough to clear my head.*

Stop.

Step one: get this job.

She forced herself to focus on preparing for her interview. She reworded and added to her work history until she was satisfied that it represented the best of what she'd done and what she could offer any employer. She printed it out, placed it in a neat folder, and put it on the counter next to her keys.

With her task completed, all that was left was to think about how rude she'd been to Lance. *If I don't apologize things will get awkward. I didn't believe I could be happy again, but I am. I can't let him ruin that.*

A memory came to her in a flash: blood running down her legs, too much to wash away in the shower. And the pain. *God, the pain.*

She closed her eyes and covered them with her hands. *Don't go there.*

Unlike Kenzi, the truth won't free me.

It'll only make me hate Lexi.

Lance.

And myself.

Enough time has gone by. Forget.

Do yourself a favor and forget.

LANCE SLAMMED THE door of his apartment behind him and dropped his keys into the small bowl he kept on the table just inside. He'd tried to call Willa back, but she hadn't answered. He didn't consider himself a vain man, but he was offended. No one brushed him off the way Willa did. He was rich, successful, and attractive. Women wanted to be with him; men wanted to network with him. Sometimes the reverse, but never did any of them treat him the way Willa did—as if he didn't matter at all.

He didn't matter enough for her to be honest with him. Not then, not now.

When given the choice between seeing him and typing up a résumé, she chose the fucking résumé.

Lance yanked off his tie and shrugged off his suit jacket. *You'd think after ten years of watching her choose to sit away rather than beside me at events, I'd learn.*

He dropped his clothing on the back of his couch and walked over to the liquor cabinet to pour himself a Scotch. He downed it in one gulp. *If she wants to work for Clay, let her.*

She's nothing more than a woman I once fucked.

The front crotch of his pants tightened instantly and he frowned. *And still want.*

After downing another shot of Scotch, Lance plopped onto the couch. He turned the television to a news channel and opened his laptop. He felt too restless to sleep. If it were earlier in the day, he would have gone for a run. Instead he'd settle for immersing himself in work.

An hour later his phone beeped with an incoming text message. He checked it absently, then sat straight up when he realized who it was from.

Sorry about tonight. I didn't mean to sound ungrateful. Thank you for offering to help me.

Lance put the phone down beside him and pinched the bridge of his nose. He shouldn't have gone to see her in the first place. If he were smart, he'd stay the hell away from her. He groaned. Ten years hadn't changed much about how he felt about her. She was still a dangerous temptation. He picked up the phone and texted back, **I shouldn't have driven over without asking if you wanted company.**

He guessed at her next words. She would smooth the situation over. Like him, she avoided emotional confrontations. That shared trait had probably been the biggest barrier to them working through whatever the hell had happened during that rollercoaster of a week in Nantucket.

That and the fact that we were so young.

Young and self-absorbed. Me, at least. I don't know who the hell she was back then. She only let me in that one time.

I shouldn't have ignored your calls. I'm interviewing for a job tomorrow, and I guess I'm nervous.

Lance swallowed hard. **What kind of job?**

Clay Landon offered me a job as his personal assistant. I've been trying unsuccessfully to find a job in the art world. This might be good for me.

Don't do it. Don't ask. **I'm starting a new project for the city. They want to revive the area around the capitol building and make it into a place where the community feels comfortable gathering for events and leisure. I could always use someone who knows what regular people like.**

When Willa didn't immediately answer, he reread his last text to her. *Shit, that came out wrong.* Lance had meant it as a compliment. Willa wasn't like the women in his social circle. She wasn't living off Daddy's money and spending her days deciding which diamond matched best with which outfit.

She was grounded. Levelheaded. The longer she went without replying, the more he felt like an ass. **I have time tomorrow morning if you'd like to meet and discuss any openings at my office.**

The moment it took her to respond felt like an eternity. **Thanks, but I have to pass on that one. Goodnight, Lance.**

Fuck.

Goodnight, Willa.

Chapter Five

WILLA STEPPED OUT of the taxi and onto the street. She clutched a folder to her chest and double-checked that she had her purse. After paying the driver she took a deep, fortifying breath and headed up the cement path that led to Dax's Boston office building. Clay had told her it was easiest for him to have their meeting there.

Her phone rang before she made it inside the building. She paused, dug through her purse for the phone, and was instantly filled with a mix of irritation and relief that it was her sister. Lexi had successfully avoided her since their argument, and it was the longest Willa had gone without speaking to her sister. Lexi had come home each night, but it had been late, and she'd left earlier than normal every morning.

"You've got an interview with Clay Landon, you hot shit." Leave it to Lexi to act as if nothing had happened between them.

Not wanting to argue and make herself even more nervous, Willa played along. "I do. Here's hoping I get it. The salary he's offering will make paying rent a breeze."

"You don't have to move out, Willa. Actually, Tessa is with Dean so much right now she said her apartment is always vacant. I might crash there for a while."

Breathe. One thing at a time. "We don't have to make any fast decisions."

Instead of addressing her last comment, Lexi said, "Kenzi told me about your interview about five minutes ago, or I would have called you sooner. Tell me you're not wearing one of your frumpy business suits."

Willa looked at her reflection in the glass door of the building and smoothed her hand down the skirt of the very outfit her sister was referring to. "I am dressed to be taken seriously."

"If you want to be taken seriously, turn your ass around, run back to our place, grab anything out of my closet and show him what he'd be saying no to if he turns you down today."

Willa rolled her eyes skyward. "First, that would make me late."

"He won't care if you pick the right dress."

"Second, I'm interviewing for a job, not a romp on his desk."

With an impatient sound, Lexi said, "Do you know how many jobs I've gotten that I wasn't qualified for simply because I choose the right outfit for the interview?"

"And how many of those jobs lasted?"

"Who cares? They paid me, didn't they? My bank never cared if I had one employer or ten. The landlord never did either. You're the only one who thinks that my way isn't good enough."

"It's not like that—" Willa sighed. *Maybe it is.* Willa stepped out of the doorway when several men walked by in suits. They didn't notice her at all. She gave her reflection another look. Her hair was tied back. She'd worn subtle makeup. "I'm not supposed to look like I'm going dancing. It's a job interview, for God's sake."

"Be careful with a man like Clay. Don't take anything he says seriously."

"What does that mean?"

Lexi sighed. "I mean if he compliments you or asks you out say no. Don't let him confuse you. I liked him when I met him, but I'm not so sure now. I don't trust him, and I don't want to see you get hurt."

"Have a little faith in me, Lexi. I'm not as naïve as you think I am."

"Good. Then get in there, get that job, and get out the minute it becomes weird. You don't owe him anything just because you agree to work for him. Remember that."

"Okay."

"And if you have your blouse buttoned up to your neck like a nun, please undo the top two."

Willa touched the top button of her blouse, which was securely closed. "Why would I want to do that?"

Lexi sighed in disgust. "I give up. Good luck with your interview."

"Thanks." Not sure what else to say, Willa hung up and turned off her phone, placing it back in her purse. She raised her chin in determination and walked into the building. *I'm going to get this job and not because of what I'm wearing.*

Once inside, she entered the elevator with several businessmen and pressed the number for her floor. She fiddled with the button near her neck. *I'm not the prude Lexi thinks I am.*

Am I?

I button my shirt up this high because it's more comfortable this way.

If I wanted to show cleavage, I could. It wouldn't bother me at all. She undid the first button and then the second. With a touch of defiance, she spread the V of the neckline open and smiled. She glanced down. The edge of her bra was still tastefully concealed.

When she raised her eyes she caught a man next to her watching her with interest. He looked about her age, but pale and soft like a man who spent too many hours at a desk. She blushed and looked away. *He probably thinks I'm stripping.*

I don't care. His opinion of me doesn't matter either.

Willa undid the third button of her shirt. It brought the V of the neckline down to the very tip of her bra. If she leaned the wrong way, she'd likely give someone quite a glimpse of her—she made a face as she remembered she'd worn a practical white cotton bra.

She raised her eyes and caught the man across from her still watching her. She glared at him. He looked away. She refastened the third button, but left the top two undone.

I'm not a prude.

Willa was relieved to step out of the elevator when it

came to the correct floor. She approached the receptionist and gave her name. "I'm here to see Mr. Landon."

The young woman gave her a puzzled look. "Do you have an appointment? He's in with Mr. Marshall at the moment."

"I have an interview."

The woman's eyebrows rose and fell. "I'll see if he's available." She held a pen above a piece of paper and looked at Willa pointedly.

"Willa Chambers."

The woman nodded, wrote the name down, then picked up the phone on her desk. "Mr. Marshall? I have a Willa Chambers here. She said she has an interview with Mr. Landon." She hung up the phone and waved a hand in the direction of a circle of chairs. "He'll be just a few minutes."

Willa nodded and took a seat. While waiting she had time to look around. The waiting area was flanked by offices. Some of the doors were open. Others were closed. These were Dax's people, and the atmosphere was fast-paced and intense. The people coming and going from the offices were all well dressed in outfits that put her department-store suit to shame. Some of the women were in outfits Lexi would have chosen. Some were dressed in slacks and blazers. They all reeked of success and money. Dax's receptionist, however, was dressed conservatively.

The door to Dax's office opened. Willa stood while Dax and Clay walked toward her. Dax smiled in greeting, but it looked forced. Clay ran a critical eye over her and made a face.

I'm not late. She looked down. *Do I have toilet paper or something stuck to my shoe? No.* She ran a hand over her hair to make sure it was still all in place and greeted them. "Dax. Mr. Landon."

"Call me Clay."

Dax sent what seemed to be a warning look at his friend. "I was just reminding Clay about how long you've known my fiancée and what a good friend you've been to her."

Willa looked back and forth between the men. It was an interesting, protective brother type of comment.

Clay held out his hand and enveloped Willa's in his. His smile was smooth. "He was threatening to disfigure me if I'm anything but a gentleman with you, but he doesn't scare me."

From Kenzi, Willa knew the two men were good friends. They probably bantered back and forth like this all the time. She tried to extricate her hand, but Clay held on to it. She pushed back a sense of panic as she remembered what Lexi had said about not taking him seriously. *He might be testing me. Well, I'll show him I'm not as timid as people think I am.* With that thought, she gave his hand a hearty squeeze.

He gave her another once-over. "I've met plenty of twins in my life, but you and your sister are spot-on identical. That's rare."

With one sharp tug, she pulled her hand free. "It's the whole 'two from the same egg' thing." She held up a manila folder. "I brought my résumé and references. Although much of my previous work was cataloguing art for an auction house, I'm excited about the opportunity to take on new responsibilities. I'm a quick student of almost any computer program. People think artists can't create spreadsheets, but I love them. You should see my grocery lists. They're alphabetized."

Clay pocketed both of his hands. "About the job I offered you."

Willa searched both men's faces. Neither looked happy. *I don't get it. Was I supposed to flirt back?* It didn't seem like Dax would have wanted her to. The whole situation was confusing.

Dax cleared his throat. "I have several entry level positions here. Kate will take you down to HR."

Willa blinked a few times quickly. *Dax doesn't want me to work for Clay.*

Clay shrugged. He was having trouble meeting her eyes. "I don't even have an office in Boston. I asked you to interview before I thought the whole thing through."

"Oh," Willa said and hugged the folder to her stomach. She told herself it was for the best. A job was a job. She should be grateful Dax had something for her.

Clay shot Dax a sullen look. "You're making me look like an asshole."

"You are an asshole," Dax countered.

"Is this better? Look at her, she's about to cry."

Thanks for making this less awkward by pointing that out. She could only imagine how her nose had reddened with emotion, and her eyes were probably all glassy with tears with a mix of embarrassment and disappointment. "I'm fine," Willa said but took a step back. "I'll come back later."

Dax barked to his secretary. "Kate, call Kenzi."

Willa shook her head and forced another bright smile. "No need. I'm perfectly fine. I just need a different résumé to apply here. I'll go home, write it up, and come back to see Kate."

Clay shook his head in amusement. "You're in trouble either way, Dax, ol' buddy. You should have let me hire her."

Willa stopped. Now that it was out in the open, she couldn't not address it. She pinned Dax down with look. "Did you ask him not to hire me?"

Dax glared at his secretary. "Now."

Kate hurriedly picked up her phone and made a call.

Why? "Why don't you want me to work for your friend?"

Clay smiled. "Yes, Dax. You've never been afraid to say it as it is. Why don't you want Willa working for me?"

Dax frowned. "Don't fuck with my family, Clay."

Eyes round, Willa watched the two powerful men bicker.

"I won't sleep with her," Clay said as if he could have if he wanted to.

Okay, that's offensive. Willa opened her mouth to say, "Damn right you won't," but neither man was paying attention to her so she swallowed her protest.

"That's not what I meant, and you know it," Dax growled. "Find something else to entertain yourself with."

Ouch. Entertain?

There was a mix of defiance and sympathy in Clay's expression. "Why don't we let her decide what she wants? Willa, I'm a royal pain in the ass. I don't make plans ahead of time unless I have to. I like to sleep until noon and work until three in the morning. There is no actual job description. All you have to do is make sure everything is where I need it to be when I need it to be there. In exchange, I'll pay you a generous salary and," he looked her over in a not so flattering way, "give you a wardrobe budget."

Deliberately ignoring the reference to her clothing, Willa considered the job. It was a job description Willa normally would have run from. Saying yes didn't make sense.

Kate called out, "Ms. Barrington said she's on her way up. She hoped to catch Ms. Chambers while she was still here so you could all go to lunch together."

With a meaningful look at his friend, Dax said, "We'll talk later, Clay."

Shaking his head in resignation, Clay said, "You're no fun." He had started to walk away when Willa found her voice.

"Wait."

Clay turned back.

"You said I could decide." She waved her folder around. It wasn't at all the job interview she'd expected, and part of her wanted to turn tail and run, but staying suddenly felt important. Like Lexi, Dax didn't think she could handle Clay. Like life, the interview wasn't living up to what she'd hoped. In the past she would have crawled home and wondered where it all went wrong, but not this time. This time she wanted to prove something to herself. "I need this job. I deserve a chance to prove I can do it. Dax, I know you think you're protecting me, but I'll be fine. I'm taking this job."

Clay smiled and raised his hands as if proclaiming his innocence. "What can I do? She hired herself."

To his secretary, Dax barked, "Make a lunch reservation for four, Kate." His eyes narrowed when he looked back at him. "Be careful, Clay. Very fucking careful."

Willa stood there, hugging the unread résumé to her. There was definitely more going on than either man wanted to explain. Clay seemed to have an agenda for offering her the job, and it was one Dax didn't approve of.

I don't care. Like Lexi said, this doesn't have to be forever. I'll get in, make some money, get out.

Willa wasn't worried that working with Clay would hurt her. In her experience, only people she loved had the power to do that.

THE LONG RUN Lance had taken that morning hadn't put him in a better mood. He'd been sitting at his office desk for a good fifteen minutes and had yet to turn on his computer. He was tired. Frustrated. Distracted. He'd spent a restless night telling himself to forget about Willa.

She didn't want anything to do with him. Was it anger or indifference? Did it matter? He'd had his chance with her, and he'd fucked it up.

I was young and stupid.
I never meant to hurt her.
I said I was sorry. Tried to make it up to her.
Ten years. Who keeps a grudge that long?

Staring blankly at his dark computer screen, he let his thoughts drift back in time. He could remember exactly how his body had clenched with excitement when she'd taken her spot on the jet ski and wrapped her arms around his waist. Ten years. He shouldn't be able to remember everywhere their bodies had touched. The feeling of her fitting herself against his back and holding on shouldn't be vivid after all the time that had passed.

Hell, he'd forgotten the names of some of the women he'd slept with over the years. He wasn't a horndog like some of his friends, but he'd been with his fair share of women. His relationships didn't last long, but he didn't expect them to, and he didn't look back after things ended.

Except with Willa. He remembered every moment with her, every brush of her hands across his body. Everything was different with her. Better.

And worse.

Lance lived his life carefully. He didn't make mistakes. He had nothing to regret.

Almost nothing.

Why can't I forget her? Because she was a virgin?

No, it's more than that.

He closed his eyes and let the memories come back to him.

It was a hot day, but the Atlantic waters were cold and rough. Every wave they crashed through drenched them both. Willa bounced behind him, her breasts moving up and down against his back. She lost her grip and cried out. He slowed and her arms wrapped around him even tighter. The back of one of her hands brushed over his hard cock. "Are you okay?" *he asked.*

"Yes," *she answered with a nervous laugh.*

"Do you want me to take you back to shore?"

She scooted closer against him. "No way. I'm loving this."

Me, too.

"Mr. Barrington, I'm covering for Ms. Cleary today." A woman's voice brought Lance back to the present. She was a mousy brunette with large, thick glasses. An unwelcomed unknown. His regular secretary was on maternity leave, and the temp agency had assured him the woman who had worked for him for the past two weeks would continue there until she returned. Apparently not.

"What's your name?" Lance asked impatiently. He was already distracted enough without adding the annoyance of training someone new.

"Ms. Niarchos."

Lance rubbed the back of his tense neck. It wasn't her fault he was having a shitty week. "Just answer the phone for now. There should be a notebook on the desk with guest log-in information. If I need anything I'll send you an email."

Instead of leaving as Lance had expected, the woman walked over to one of his bookshelves and picked up a notebook. "I used to have a journal just like this."

"Please don't touch anything in my office." With a few purposeful strides, Lance was beside her, taking his aunt's journal out of her hands. Her eyes narrowed slightly, then her expression went blank again. Lance was detail-oriented. It's what gave him an advantage with people as well as architecture. There was something about her that didn't fit with the way she presented herself. He'd heard of architect firms planting informants in the offices of their competitors, but he'd never come across it in person. He dismissed the thought as paranoid. "I left some envelopes on your desk this morning. Please make sure they get in the post by noon."

"Absolutely." The woman smiled again but didn't turn to leave. "Have you read it?"

Lance looked down at the journal in his hand. It had belonged to his mother's sister, Patrice. Emily had read it and thought some of the entries were disturbing enough that she'd wanted to ask Sophie about them. Lance and Kenzi had decided it was better if they read the journal themselves. Kenzi said she'd found nothing but the ramblings of an old woman. Lance hadn't read past the first few pages. He'd never known his aunt and had no interest in reading about her life. "No." He turned and put it on his desk.

The secretary met his eyes boldly. "You should. The one I had was chock-full of scandalous secrets. I've always wondered why people write things down if they don't want anyone to know about them. People can't help it, I suppose. If they know something, they can't keep it to themselves."

The whole conversation felt odd, so Lance ended it. "That'll be all, Ms. Niarchos."

"Of course, Mr. Barrington." With that, she left his office, closing the door behind her. Lance returned to his desk and started his computer. On impulse he opened the cover of the journal. Inside he found a black business card that hadn't been there before. All it had on it was a white phone number. He closed the journal and strode to the door. His secretary was no longer at her desk. Irritated he called down to the Human Resources department to ask where she was.

He felt an unusual sensation of unease when he was told there'd been a mix up with the temp agency. No secretary had been sent that day, but one would be there within the hour.

"Then who the hell is Ms. Niarchos?" Lance asked impatiently.

"I'm sorry, who?"

He called down to his security desk and told them that an unauthorized person had been in his office. He wanted IDs checked and a copy of the security tapes for his floor. He was even less happy a few minutes later when the head of his security informed him that there was a glitch in the camera system that morning. Nothing had been recorded.

None of it made sense. Yes, he'd just gotten a huge contract with the city of Boston, but that wasn't a secret. He picked up the black business card and called the number on it. When he heard someone answer he said, "Who the hell are you?"

"Who I am doesn't matter."

"It does when you pretend to work for me. Is this some kind of joke?"

"No, but what you consider a security system is."

"If I catch you in my building again—"

An unapologetic laugh. "Don't threaten me, Mr. Barrington. Just read your aunt's journal."

What the hell? "What are you talking about?"

"I'd do the legwork for you, but I'm trying not to get involved. I have to say, though, I'm a little disappointed in your family's lack of curiosity." The line went dead. When

Lance tried to call it back it rang through to a voicemail box that was full.

He called again but no one answered. *What the hell?*

Lance ran a hand through his hair. If the day wasn't already crazy enough, it had just taken a bizarre turn. He sat down and opened the journal with the intention of reading it when his phone beeped from an incoming text.

Kenzi. **Having lunch at the Bancroft with Dax, Clay, and Willa. She took the job.**

No. Not going to happen. Lance dropped the journal into his computer bag, sent out an email to cancel his one o'clock meeting, and strode out of his office.

He sped across town to the restaurant, tossed his keys to a valet, and only slowed his pace once he entered the restaurant. He spotted Willa almost instantly and went to the table without stopping to speak to the hostess.

Kenzi stood when she saw him, "Lance, what a great surprise."

So that's how we play this? Okay. He gave her a quick kiss on the cheek. "I was about to have lunch alone. Mind if I join you?" He shook Dax's hand in greeting.

"We'd love that," Kenzi exclaimed.

Lance pulled a chair over from another table and placed it between Clay and Willa. He accepted a menu from a server and ordered a quick sandwich since the others already had plates of food in front of them. After handing the menu to the server, he looked at Willa, but she didn't meet his gaze. It gave him a moment to appreciate the simple beauty of her. Her hair was neatly pulled back, exposing the delicate, delicious curve of her neck. His eyes widened as he noted the delicious way her blouse was undone. From where he was he could see the curve of her breast. Would it still fill his hand perfectly as it had all those years ago?

"What brought you to this side of town?" Clay asked drolly.

Step one: keep Clay and Willa in Boston. "Clay. I'm starting a preliminary assessment of the city properties abutting the capitol building. I could use your experience with modernizing the historic ones to code." Lance accepted a glass of water from the server.

Kenzi sat forward. "I thought you said—" Her eyes darted around the table, and she dropped what she was about to say and instead said, "That's fantastic." She turned to her friend. "Willa, you love old buildings. I bet you'd also be an asset to the project."

Willa looked across at Clay. "I'm sure I'll be too busy to add anything else to my plate yet." With her hands still carefully folded, she directed her next comment to Lance. "I read an article about the Capitol Complex. It's a daunting responsibility."

"I like a challenge," Lance said while looking her directly in the eye. The air was charged with the sexual tension that was always present with Willa. Even something as simple as sitting next to her in a restaurant was enough to set his heart beating wildly in his chest. When she shifted in her chair, her leg brushed against his briefly, and he could have sworn it affected her as much as it did him. He cleared his throat and thought about which parts of the project might lure her to it.

"It's more than just renovating buildings; it's creating another place for people to come together. Not commercial. The city wants to celebrate the diversity of the community. My task will be to weave the past with the present in a way that showcases Boston's history while valuing the flavor of what it represents today."

Kenzi added, "The project could change the heart of the city for generations to come. Wouldn't it be amazing to be part of something like that, Willa?"

Willa looked down at her plate as if to compose herself then said, "I'm sure it would."

Clay took a sip of his wine before saying, "Too bad she already has a job."

Dax ordered a shot of whiskey.

Lance tensed, but forced his tone to remain calm. "Working for you, Clay?"

"Yes," Clay said, twirling his glass between this fingers. "She's my personal assistant."

"What happened to your last one?" Lance asked between gritted teeth.

Clay shrugged. "Never had one. Didn't think I needed one." His eyes lingered on Willa's face for longer than Lance liked. "Until I heard Willa was looking for work."

Lance's hand clenched around his napkin. He wanted to tell Willa she couldn't take the job, but he knew he didn't have that right. He wanted to feed the napkin to Clay, but out of respect for Dax he wouldn't do that either. In what he hoped was a calm voice, Lance said, "I can't imagine Willa being happy for long with something that wasn't art related.

My project includes designing murals for the community center. I was serious with my earlier offer, Willa. I could use your input."

Willa pressed her lips together briefly, then asked, "Because I know what average people like?"

Ouch. That comment hadn't taken long to come back and bite him in the ass. "Regular people," he corrected. "And I meant it as a compliment."

Clay coughed to cover a comment that was still audible. "Not better."

Kenzi leaned toward Willa. "What Lance is trying to say is that you have a style that appeals to a great number of people."

A pink flush crept up Willa's neck. "I appreciate that, but as Clay said, I have a job."

Pushing the subject further would have put everyone at the table in an awkward position. What he wanted to say to Willa wouldn't first be voiced in public. He decided to move onto another subject that was occupying his thoughts. "Something happened at my office this morning." He shared the story of the woman who had posed as his secretary and the odd card she'd left.

Dax frowned. "How the hell did she get by your security?"

Lance grimaced. "I never needed that much. I'm an architect. I don't have enemies."

When Dax arched an eyebrow, Lance added, "No offense."

"None taken," Dax said easily. "I assume you'll be making major changes."

"I'm having IDs checked and looking into what happened with the video cameras."

"That's not enough. I'll make a few calls," Dax said firmly.

"That won't be necessary," Lance countered.

"I disagree," Dax said, sounding uncomfortably similar to Lance's older brothers. He took out a phone and sent a text.

Lance almost told Dax where he could shove his phone then he saw his sister reach for her fiancé's hand and thank him. She'd found someone who truly made her happy. For her, he'd put his irritation aside.

Sounding as if he was repeating his question, Clay asked, "What's in the journal?"

Lance shrugged. "Kenzi read more of it than I did."

Kenzi's expression turned apologetic. "I didn't get through much." She looked at Dax, her eyes glowing in a way that made Lance look away. "I've been busy."

He turned his attention to his future brother-in-law. "Did you find anything, Dax?"

Although he didn't answer, the look he gave Lance said, "Are you fucking serious?"

"What happened to all of us reading it?" Even as Lance voiced his complaint, he knew he couldn't blame them. He hadn't been able to get past the third page.

"I'll look at it if you want," Willa interjected. "I love to read."

Lance's eyes flew to hers. He was wise enough to know

that sometimes life handed a person an opportunity. He wouldn't have become successful in his career if he didn't recognize and capitalize on them. "Perfect. It's in my office. Why don't I drop by your place tonight? We can look it over together."

Willa opened her mouth to say something, then shut it. He could tell she wanted to retract her offer, but Kenzi was already thanking her. "No need to go out of your way. I can pick it up on my way to work tomorrow." She turned to Clay. "Did you want me to start tomorrow?"

"Sure," Clay said with a flash of a smile. "How about noon?"

"Noon? Really? Where should I meet you?" Willa asked, looking confused.

"At my hotel. You could come earlier, but I'll still be in bed." He winked.

That's it. Lance's hand clenched into fists. Between gritted teeth he said, "Since you'll be consulting on my project, Clay, we should all meet at my office. I'll go over the plans with you before we tour the proposed buildings."

With a lift and drop of a shoulder, Clay answered in a bored tone, "Sounds tedious, but I did agree to help you."

In the same authoritative voice he'd used earlier, Dax said, "You'll need a base in Boston, Clay. I have several empty offices in my building. Conduct the rest of your business there." His tone had a warning edge to it.

Clay agreed with an amused nod.

Lance looked back and forth between the two men. Did Dax know his friend was a douche? If so, why had he allowed

Clay to offer her a job in the first place?

Kenzi was staring up at Dax with blatant adoration. He appeared just as smitten with her. It was a bit much to stomach.

Lance glanced at Willa and lost his train of thought when their eyes met. There was a spark of something in her eyes that he hadn't seen in a long time. Desire? Excitement?

He couldn't say or do much while they had an audience.

But they wouldn't the next morning.

Chapter Six

THE NEXT MORNING, a half-dressed Willa stood in the hallway of her apartment, wavering between her bedroom and Lexi's. Lexi hadn't come home the night before, but she'd texted that she was staying at Tessa's apartment. Willa had responded that she'd taken the job with Clay. Lexi had sent back a thumbs-up. It wasn't a fulfilling exchange, but at least they were talking.

She hadn't said anything about seeing Lance that morning. He was still too volatile a subject with them. It was killing Willa to not be able to ask Kenzi for her advice, either. Willa had other friends, but none as close. None she would call before work and ask something like this.

What do I wear on my first day of work at a job without a clear description? And to see Lance? I shouldn't care what he thinks of how I look.

But I do.

She thought about the comment Clay had made about giving her a wardrobe budget and sighed. She headed into Lexi's room. *She does have excellent taste.*

Willa tried on what looked like a simple blue dress. It

was sleeveless and from the front it had a classic, demure neckline. Her eyes popped, however, when she spun and caught a glimpse of the back of the dress in the mirror. The material clung to her curves and the hemline was short, but not indecent. She frowned. The dip in the back of the dress, however, made underwear tricky. She stripped it off and tossed it on Lexi's bed.

She chose a cream skirt and peach blouse next. The skirt fit her well, but the blouse showed too much cleavage and made Willa want to safety pin it closed. It certainly wasn't appropriate for a work setting.

It would certainly get Lance's attention.

Shaking her head, Willa took it off. *I don't want that. Do I?*

Her body tingled with the memory of how he'd looked at her the night before. She remembered that look—that hunger. A much younger Lance had looked at her the same way, and she'd spent years trying to forget where it had led.

Memories flooded back. *She was eighteen again, standing before a mirror indecisively. She'd spent the most amazing day with Lance. He'd taken her out on his jet ski then stayed with her most of the day. They'd played volleyball, sat next to each other during lunch, and taken a long walk together. Willa remembered the first time he reached for her hand. A light exploded within her—a joy beyond what words could express.*

Still in their bathing suits, they walked to the end of the beach and found themselves temporarily away from the others. For what felt like an eternity they simply stared into each other's eyes. Desire clearly burned in Lance's eyes, but something held him back.

"Are you seeing anyone?" Willa asked and held her breath while waiting for his answer.

"No, you?"

"No one." She didn't think being that happy was possible—at least not for her. The man she'd spent two years dreaming about was looking down at her as if he felt the same about her.

He cupped her face between his hands. "You're so beautiful."

In that moment Willa felt beautiful. She was also beyond choosing her words carefully. "You, too."

His chuckle was the sexiest thing she'd ever heard. His expression turned serious. "We shouldn't do this. I told myself I wouldn't. I'm a junior in college, Willa. You're barely out of high school."

Do what? Hold hands? Date? Be seen together? His comment stung. She pulled away from him. "If you don't want to be with me, then don't be with me."

His expression turned tormented, and he pulled her into his arms. Their first kiss. It blew away anything she'd experienced before. It was bold, sexual, and an expression of his hunger for her. She wrapped her arms around his neck, arched against him, and gave herself over to how good kissing him felt. His hands ran over her, as demanding as his kiss and just as pleasurable. His bare chest was heaven beneath her hands. She'd dated boys in high school. A few of them had gotten overly excited from kissing, and she found their lack of control scary.

It wasn't like that with Lance. Her brain spun as every nerve ending in her body was overwhelmed and pulsed a request for more—more Lance. She didn't feel like a virgin. She felt like a woman drowning beneath wave after wave of her own desire.

Kissing him felt as essential as air.

When he pulled back, she felt the loss with confusing intensity. She stood there, with one hand on her mouth, simply staring up at him as they both fought to catch their breath.

"I want to be with you," he said, his voice husky and deep. "Too much." He let out a long, shaky breath and looked around. "I forgot that we're not alone. You're dangerous."

Dangerous? Willa had never been described that way. She was the careful one, the quiet one, the one people overlooked. She didn't care who was watching or what they were thinking. She wanted to be the woman she saw in Lance's eyes. "I want to be with you, too."

Lance shuddered. Willa thought he'd pull her back into his arms, but instead he took her hand again. "We need to walk."

Willa fell into step beside him. She tried to figure out what was holding him back. "I may be young, but I've been on my own for years. I'm not a child."

He'd stopped and pinned her down with those incredible dark eyes of his. "Are you a virgin?"

"Yes," she admitted, unable to lie to him.

"Fuck," he said and started walking again.

Offended, Willa said, "It's not a disease, you know."

He frowned as they walked hand in hand down the beach in the direction of his family's house. "You're Kenzi's best friend. I can't do this."

She'd pulled him to a stop. Not many of her friends had graduated with their virginity intact. Losing it had been a badge of honor to some. To others it had been an impulsive poor choice. Willa had always maintained that sex should wait until a woman was with someone she loved.

"Because I'm a virgin? Okay, I'll go to college, sleep with someone else, and we'll try this again next summer."

His grip on her hand became painful. "Don't."

"Don't sleep with someone else?" she'd asked, hoping her prod was working.

He took both of her shoulders in his hands and looked her directly in the eye. "Don't push me to do something we'll both regret. I'm trying to make the right choice here."

Rejection was a kick in the ass. Willa mustered her strength and held his gaze. "And what is the right choice?"

He cupped a side of her face. "I don't know. I can't think when I'm with you."

"I know exactly what you mean," she agreed. When he looked at her like that, there was nothing beyond him and how he made her feel.

Willa's phone rang, bringing her fully back to the present. She let the call ring through as she slowly extricated herself from the heady memories. Even after all the time that had passed, those memories had the power to make her heart pound and her body warm.

Still in just her cotton panties and bra, Willa sat down on Lexi's bed beside the mound of clothing she'd tried on. She silently repeated a mantra she'd used many times over the last decade. *Forget. It only hurts when I let myself remember.*

Her phone rang again. Willa looked down at it and smiled sadly. Kenzi always knew when she needed her. It was a joke between Willa and Lexi that Kenzi had somehow tapped into their twin connection. "Good morning."

"It is a good morning. You not only have a job, but you're also going to see Lance."

"I'm interested to see what's in that journal." She held back her true feelings. Willa was close enough to Kenzi to consider her like a sister, but Lance was a subject they'd always avoided. Kenzi had grown up in a family where people didn't push for the truth. It had taken a long time before she'd felt comfortable enough with Willa and Lexi to even express when she was upset.

Kenzi was changing, though. The more she spent with her fiancé, Dax, the blunter she became. Willa was still trying to decide how she felt about it.

"That's what you're excited about today?" Kenzi asked with a hint of humor in her voice.

Willa paced her bedroom restlessly. "And starting my new job."

"There isn't anything else you want to talk about?"

"Like what?"

"Like Lance."

Willa froze. "What about him?"

Kenzi sighed audibly. "Willa, it's me. Do you really think I don't know that you like my brother?"

"Of course I like him. I like your whole family."

Kenzi was quiet for a moment, then she said, "Did you see Lance's face when he thought you were going to meet Clay at his hotel? He wanted to forbid you to go."

Willa walked to her closet and absently began to sift through potential outfits. "Your brothers have always been overprotective." It was true to a point. Kenzi's brothers had always hovered over their sister, but they'd always carefully kept their distance from her friends.

"Do you have health insurance?"

Willa held up a modest, tan pantsuit and considered it. "Yes. I've kept coverage while job hunting. Why?"

"Because I'm about to slap you into next Tuesday."

Willa's jaw dropped open, and she replaced the suit. She was momentarily speechless in the face of Kenzi's comment. In all the years they'd been friends, Kenzi had never spoken to her that way.

Kenzi continued, "I'm sorry, Willa, but I'm done keeping my thoughts to myself in fear that people won't like what I have to say. I won't live like that again. I don't care if you like my brother or not, but I do care that you won't be honest with me about it. Tell everyone else that today isn't important to you, but don't lie to me."

Willa covered her face with one hand for a moment, then lowered it and said quietly, "I've been trying to decide what to wear for the last hour."

"Have you looked in Lexi's closet?"

Willa winced as her ego took another hit. For a long time, Willa had turned her back on everything Lexi represented. Somehow she'd lost a piece of herself when she did that. It was one thing to be shy, it was another to feel trapped by your own fears. She didn't want to go back to who she was, but she also didn't know how to move forward. She remembered a time, before their parents had died, when she'd felt as loved and lovable as Lexi. Losing them had shaken her, and somewhere along the way she'd lost her confidence. *On the outside I'm just as beautiful as Lexi. How do I find my way back to feeling that way?*

I'm smart. At least smart enough to have gotten my degree. I'm hardworking. I've made my own money for as long as I can remember. On paper, I have my shit together.

I wish I saw that person when I look in the mirror. "I did. Nothing feels right."

She waited for Kenzi to suggest she wear something from her designer wardrobe, but she didn't. Instead she asked, "Have you tried mixing your styles?"

Willa thought about the skirt she'd tried on that she'd liked. She took one of her favorite blouses out of her closet and smiled for the first time that day. "You're a genius, Kenzi."

Kenzi chuckled. "No, I just know you. Both of you. I can't wait to see what you choose. Will you send me a picture of it?"

Not hanging up, Willa shrugged on the blouse then sprinted to her sister's room, found the skirt she'd liked, and pulled it on as well. She looked at the huge pile of clothing on Lexi's bed, then at the time on the clock beside it, and grimaced. *I'll put it all away before she gets back, but right now I'm out of time.* She dug through Lexi's closet for a pair of shoes with a moderate heel. She snapped a photo of herself and sent it to Kenzi. "What do you think?"

"Perfect, but you have your hair done up like you're a librarian."

"That's how I always wear it. It stays out of my way." *Or does it help me hide better? Is Lexi right about that?*

"How about a looser knot?"

Willa walked back into her bathroom and placed the phone down so she could undo her hair. She pulled it back, but let it drop when she didn't like how it looked. She swept it up again, this time leaving a few wisps free around her face and secured it. She took a quick selfie and sent it to Kenzi.

"You look awesome, Willa."

"Really?" On impulse, Willa applied a darker lipstick color than she normally wore. She also applied a hint more eyeliner. She sent one final picture. "What about this?"

"Oh, my God. Your eyes look fantastic. You should do them like that all the time."

Willa smiled down at the phone. She thought, *Good friends accept you as you are; best friends do, too, but they will also kick your ass when you need it. No matter how lost you get, they are right there, showing you the way back.* "Kenzi, all I'm doing is picking up a journal from your brother's office."

"Promise me something?"

"Depends on what it is."

"I don't know what happened between you and Lance when we were younger, but none of us are who we were back then. Give yourself a chance to get to know who he is now."

Willa agreed to because not doing so would have opened a conversation she wasn't ready to have. Kenzi was right about one thing, though, Willa wasn't who she'd been at eighteen.

I'm a hell of a lot wiser.

I know now that sex doesn't mean the same thing to everyone. Sometimes it doesn't mean anything at all.

Lust and love are two very different things.
And confusing them is a devastating mistake I won't make again.

LANCE PACED HIS office while waiting for Willa to arrive. He'd directed his secretary to buzz him the moment she arrived. Unable to concentrate on anything else, he'd called down to the building's security desk and told them to call him when Willa arrived.

He was on edge and had lain awake most of the night, planning exactly how he'd approach the subject of the past. His goal wasn't to prove who had been right and who'd been wrong. If he played their meeting right he would finally have answers to questions that had plagued him for a decade.

Then, hopefully, they could move past it.

An image of her gasping with pleasure as he pounded into her filled his mind, overwhelmed his senses for a moment. He wanted her so badly he could practically taste her.

This isn't just about fucking her.
Although that's part of it.

His hands clenched at his sides. He liked to think he was a better man than he'd been at twenty. His brothers had warned him that being with Kenzi's friends would end badly, but back then how Willa made him feel was more important than who she was. He'd had ten years to regret letting his dick override his decision to respect her relationship with his family.

I could have done everything better. I could have waited,

gotten to know her. Who the hell knows where it might have gone? She shouldn't have been a one-night stand.

Not Willa.

Over the years he'd witnessed her unwavering loyalty to his sister and his family. Her gentle heart made it impossible for anyone to not want the best for her. She had a gift of making everyone, even his often miserable family, feel better. Like him, she smoothed situations over rather than added drama. She was genuinely a good person. Someone who liked kids, animals, old people. Hell, he'd never seen her express a dislike of anyone.

Besides me.

I was a class A prick.

Lance rubbed one hand roughly across his forehead and let the memories in.

He was back in the guest cottage with her lying naked in his arms on the bed. Her head was on his shoulder and she was smiling, but he was losing his mind. He didn't know if he should stay, leave, apologize, or just grab his pants and run. Not only had he just fucked his little sister's best friend, but the condom had broken. That had never happened to him before. Of course, he hadn't planned to have sex during a family vacation, so he'd used the emergency condom he'd tucked into his wallet years earlier. He wasn't the type to impulsively jump into bed with women. He was a careful and considerate partner. It was something his college friends sometimes teased him about, but he knew that actions had consequences and sometimes they lasted a lifetime.

He wanted to blame the beers he'd had with Andrew after

Willa had gone up to the house with Kenzi and Lexi. He knew, though, that the slight buzz he'd had when Willa returned alone had been gone before they'd sought privacy in the guest house.

The sex itself had been good. So fucking good he wanted her again. Had it been good for her? He hoped so. Despite how he'd felt, he'd tried to go slowly, be gentle. In the end, she'd wrapped herself around him and the sex had taken a wild, uncontrolled life of its own. They'd collapsed, sweaty and spent, onto the bed and only then had he realized the fragile nature of old latex.

Fuck.

He'd cleaned himself off and had been gathering his thoughts when she'd snuggled up against him. He knew he had to tell her, but she looked so happy, so damn innocent guilt twisted his gut. He turned onto his side so he was face to face with her. "Willa, what we just did was—"

"Amazing," she finished his sentence and caressed a side of his face with her hand. "I'm glad I waited. So glad my first time was with you."

There was a special place in hell waiting for him. Lance was sure. He cleared his throat and took her hand in his. "There's something you need to know."

Her face crumpled. "Are you seeing someone?"

"No. No. Nothing like that."

The smile returned to her face. "Sorry." She pulled her hand free from his and wiped at her eyes. "I'm being an idiot."

"You're not. Not at all."

"You're just saying that to make me feel better. You're like that—always making sure everyone is okay. Kenzi is lucky to have a brother like you."

There it was again, that trust in him he didn't deserve. He

remembered something his father had told him when he'd explained the facts of life to him. He hadn't focused on the mechanics of it so much as the etiquette and responsibility of choosing to be sexually active. "If you're not comfortable enough with someone to discuss contraception, you don't know them well enough to sleep with."

Sound advice, Dad. But you left out the possibility of the male brain completely shutting down long enough to make a mistake like this.

"Willa, I'm not good at talking about things like this, but—"

A huge smile spread across her face. "I love you, too."

Lance sat straight up. "What?"

She sat up next to him. "I think I've loved you since the first time I met you. I knew I was too young, but I'm not any more. We can be together now."

Oh, shit. It wasn't that Lance didn't like Willa. He did. But she was giving what they'd done an importance he hadn't considered. In her eyes he saw a terrifying truth—she thought what they'd done meant they were in a relationship.

Not a dating relationship. Not one with a trial period. No, she was all in. One hundred percent. Whatever he felt for her was overshadowed by panic.

I'm not ready to love anyone. Not like that.

And the broken condom? What if something comes from this?

I can't ask her to terminate a pregnancy if one happens. I don't believe in abortions.

Do I?

If I don't, and she gets pregnant, I'm fucked.

Trapped.

He stood up and grabbed his clothing from the floor. Once he had his pants on again and was buttoning up his shirt, he began to calm. By then, though, she'd had time to realize he hadn't responded to her declaration. She was clutching a sheet to the front of her and her eyes were brimming with tears.

Lance finished buttoning his shirt and sat on the edge of the bed. Instead of reaching for her, he faced away from her with his hands hanging between his knees and his shoulders slumped. "The condom broke, Willa. There's something called a morning-after pill. I'm thinking you should take one. Unless you're on birth control already . . ."

Her hand touched his shoulder. "I'm not, but is that why you're upset? It's okay."

"No, it's not," he snapped and cursed under his breath.

Willa was quiet for several moments, then he heard her move to leave the bed. "I should go."

He turned and watched her hastily gather her clothing. She was crying. He stood, walked over to her and reached out a hand to her. She moved away from him, refusing to look at him. He hated that he'd hurt her. He felt like he'd failed her.

He wanted to tell her she'd misunderstood. He wanted to tell her that he loved her, too, and that it had been that way since he'd first met her. But that would have been a lie.

He liked her.

His body craved hers.

But love?

He didn't know anything about love. He was still trying to figure himself and his career path out. He couldn't add anyone else to that equation. Not yet.

The best he could do was be honest with her. "I'm sorry,

Willa."

She angrily adjusted her clothing and met his eyes. Her tone was angry and tears were pouring down her cheeks. "Don't be. Now I can go to college unencumbered by my virginity. Really, you did me a favor."

He hated the idea of her with anyone else as much as he hated seeing her upset. He pulled her into his arms. "I'm an ass."

She struggled at first then stood there as he held her against him. He felt the tension rippling through her.

He rested his chin on her forehead. "I don't like the idea of you with anyone else."

She sniffed but refused to look up at him. "Is that supposed to make me feel better?"

"It's the truth. I'm freaking out on the inside, Willa. Maybe that makes me an awful person. I don't know. I didn't plan any of this. You deserve better."

She let out a shaky breath. "Do I?"

Lance cursed his body for sending his blood rushing back to his dick. He didn't want to want her right then. He wanted to find the words to make her feel better. Coherent thought was difficult, however, when his cock was jerking in his pants, begging to be freed. The feel of her against him, the scent of her, the lingering taste of her on his lips was almost too much for him to resist. He kissed her temple and murmured, "Can we start over? Spend the day together tomorrow?"

Her eyes rose to his. "Like a date?"

She looked hopeful, and he resented the way it made him feel. Guilt was a tool people used as leverage to control each other. He wasn't looking for another situation where another person's vulnerability essentially trapped him.

Then stay the fuck away from her.

It wasn't that simple. A person doesn't decide to breathe. It's not something they think about either, until they're somehow deprived of being able to. Then it's all that matters. Lance wasn't ready for what Willa represented, but the idea of losing her was even worse.

"Call it whatever you want. We'll take the ferry to Martha's Vineyard. I'll show you around." *Get the hell away from my family.*

There was a kindness in her expression, an easy forgiveness, that had him almost retracting his invitation. "I'd like that."

"Come on, I'll walk you back."

The door of Lance's office opened and his temp secretary stuck her head in. "Mr. Barrington? I hate to disturb you, but I tried to buzz you . . ."

Lance shook off the past. "I didn't hear it. What is it?"

"Miss Chambers is on her way up."

Letting out a slow breath, Lance nodded. "Send her in as soon as she arrives."

If nothing else came from their meeting that morning, Lance was determined to find out why Willa had sent Lexi in her place for their date.

Why not just say she didn't want to see him?

Why the lies?

And if she cared so little about him that she could play him like that, why was she still upset with him?

He'd told himself the answers to those questions weren't as important as keeping the peace in his family. She'd told him to leave her alone and he had.

He might have been able to continue to, but then she'd lied to him again. This time she'd pretended to be Lexi. And the way she'd danced for him. He'd fought for years to not think about how it had been with her, but watching her shake her ass defiantly at him had brought it all back again.

She wouldn't leave his office until he at least knew what the hell had happened ten years ago.

Chapter Seven

WILLA BARELY HEARD what Lance's secretary was saying, but she followed her to his office door anyway. Willa's heart was thudding loudly in her chest. She tried to tell herself she was only there to pick up the journal.

She'd been very careful to never be alone with Lance—ever. She kept her distance and did her best to forget. It was the only way she'd been able to move on. *Or try to.*

He opened the door to his office, and Willa's pace faltered. If their brief history bothered him at all, it had never shown on his face. Ever since she'd told him she never wanted to talk to him again, his expression had been carefully neutral.

Worse than hating her, he'd shown indifference.

He didn't, however, look indifferent right then. There was a hunger burning in his eyes that tugged at her old feelings for him. She didn't want to feel anything around him, but the chemistry they'd always shared was impossible to deny.

Which means nothing.
Animals mate indiscriminately.

People have evolved past letting their genitalia make decisions for them.

Her inner self-lecture did nothing to lessen how her body hummed with anticipation as she walked toward him. He held out his hand to shake hers and she froze. She didn't want to touch him, didn't want their connection to deepen. She knew exactly how good it would feel.

That kind of good had almost destroyed her once. Never again.

Still, to prove to herself that she was now in control of her attraction to him, she placed her hand in his and met his eyes. "I don't want to take up your time. If you have the journal, I'll take it and go."

His hold on her lingered. "Tell me, what do you think of the building?"

Honestly, Willa hadn't noticed much about it. Her thoughts had revolved around their meeting. She based her answer on a general impression of it. "It serves its purpose, I suppose, but—"

"But? Don't hold back on my account." His hand tightened on hers.

She pried her hand out of his. "It lacks warmth."

He frowned and motioned for her to follow him inside his office. She did, and he closed the door behind her. He led the way to a glass table with a pair of stark white chairs beside it. "It's not a home, it's a place of business." She took one of the seats, and he sat across from her. "It has been lauded in several architectural magazines as a glimpse into the future."

"How depressing," Willa said without thinking, then bit her lip. She didn't come to fight with him. "Sorry. I shouldn't have said that."

He held her gaze intently. "What would you change about it?"

Willa lifted and dropped a shoulder. His questions were about more than the building. She knew she shouldn't respond, but it was tempting to tell him what she thought in terms of his building. "The exterior is striking, but there isn't anything unique about the interior. No grand foyer at its heart. Nothing that makes a person feel welcome when they enter. Nothing that would make them want to return."

"I optimized the space available. Adding a foyer would have wasted most of the ground floor."

"It's only my opinion. You seem happy with your design. What I think doesn't matter."

Lance leaned forward. "That's where you're wrong. It does. It always has."

Willa shook her head. She rejected how good his words made her feel. Even if he felt that way, it was too little too late. She wasn't a good enough liar, even to herself, to be with him and pretend he hadn't almost destroyed her. She didn't want to go back to feeling the way she had after being with him. It had been a low point in her life. Others had disappointed her in the past, but that year she'd added her own name to those who had let her down. Forcing levity into her tone, she asked, "So, where is this infamous journal?"

He rested his elbows on his knees and held her eyes. "Do

you realize this is the first time we've been alone since Nantucket? Ten years."

Willa swallowed hard. The child in her wanted to run from the room. The woman in her wanted to prove to him he didn't matter enough for her to run. "Has it been that long? God, we're getting old fast."

"You still owe me an explanation."

The attraction she felt for him fell to the wayside and fury surged through her. She'd thought she could do it. She'd thought enough time had passed, but it hadn't. When the Band-Aid of denial was ripped off, the wound was still fresh. She shot to her feet. "I owe you nothing." She turned to leave but he was in front of her, blocking her exit. "Get out of my way. It was a mistake to come here."

He grabbed one of her arms and held it painfully. "The mistake was waiting this long to talk it out. I deserve to know what happened. Why are you still angry with me? You wanted to have sex that night as much as I did. I didn't take advantage of you."

The room spun, and Willa gripped the back of one of the chairs to steady herself. Memories of that night were still painful as they tore through her. "You're hurting my arm," she said, pulling at her arm.

He relaxed his hold, but didn't release her. "Look at me, Willa."

She did and his expression turned tormented. She couldn't hide her anger from him. It was no longer worth trying to deny it was there. "I thought I could do this, Lance, but I can't."

"Why?" his asked in a tight voice. "Was it that bad?"

The absurdity of the question made her laugh sadly. "The sex? No, the sex was fine." Some of her fury was replaced by deep sadness. There was no way back. Explaining why wouldn't make either of them feel better. "The past is done and gone. Let it go."

He shook his head. "I can't. Why did you send Lexi on the date the next day? I know I didn't handle myself well after we—"

"Fucked?" she asked harshly, using the vulgar description to trivialize what they'd done.

Lance waved his free hand in the air. "I was twenty with more hormones than brains. But I liked *you*. I didn't realize it was Lexi until it was too late."

This time Willa did pull free. "Exactly, you didn't realize it was Lexi. You even kissed her. Maybe more. Honestly, I don't care." Willa stepped away to leave, but Lance blocked her path again.

"Yes, I kissed her. She said she was you. She was in your fucking clothes. I was out of my mind confused already. The last thing I expected was for you to send someone else in your place. Why did you?"

Willa crossed her arms protectively across herself. *Is that what he thought? That I sent her?* She thought back to the hateful things he'd said to her the next time he'd seen her. He'd called her immature and had gone on and on about how wrong he'd been to think he could be with someone like her. At the time she'd thought he was referring to her declaration of love, but had the switch hurt him as well?

She'd never considered that possibility. "I didn't send her. Lexi told me you needed to do something for your father that day. I believed her."

Lance brought a hand to his forehead. "Why would she do that?"

Blinking back tears, Willa shook with emotion. "Maybe she thought she was protecting me from you. She was suspicious that something had happened between us. Or maybe she wanted to prove she could have you too, if she wanted. I used to care about the real reason, but I don't anymore. And asking the questions only makes it hurt more."

"I didn't know, Willa."

"You should have." *I gave you everything. My body. My heart. How could you kiss every inch of me and not see that it was Lexi the next day?*

His shoulders slumped a little. "I'm sorry. It was stupid. I can't change what happened. But I am—I'm sorry. How long can you hate me for something I did ten years ago?"

His apology was a torment of its own. If only it had ended with Lexi pretending to be her and him not knowing the difference. She could have forgiven him for that.

I don't hate you. This would be so much easier if I did.

SHE COVERED HER face with one hand. "When she came back and told me you'd kissed her, a piece of me died. I know you think it was a ridiculous case of puppy love, but it was more than that. For me, at least. It was more. Then you were so angry."

"Shit, Willa. I don't know what else to say. I was young and self-absorbed. I felt like a fool when I thought you'd sent your sister in your place." He took the hand away from her eyes gently. "I said stupid things."

Still holding his hand, Willa felt his tension. His regret was sincere. It made what she knew she had to do even harder. Reliving that time, even briefly, had shaken her deeply. She'd once judged Sophie for hanging on to a loss so tightly her family paid for it. That kind of pain had been inconceivable to Willa until she'd experienced a loss of her own and discovered there were wounds that time doesn't heal. *Can't heal.*

And some held the terrifying power of ripping everything away from a person.

She'd come to a truce, if not peace, with herself. She'd survived. Her relationship with Lexi was still intact. Hell, they still shared an apartment together. She wouldn't allow the past to continue to hurt her. *Moving forward, Willa.* It was better for all of them if Lance thought she was upset because of mistaken identity. There was no need for him to know . . . Intent on keeping the rest to herself, she said, "It's okay, Lance. It was a long time ago. We were both young, and maybe that's all we're guilty of." This time she gently removed her hand from his. "We'll probably always be part of each other's lives, but that's all there can ever be for us."

Lance cupped one side of her face with his hand. "Then what do we do with this?" His mouth came down and claimed hers.

Despite everything she'd said, every shred of sanity she'd

clung to, she opened her lips for him. She met his plundering kiss with a frenzy that came from years of pent-up hunger. Hunger *for him*. She gripped his strong shoulders and gave herself over to a passion that burned hotter than any she'd experienced with other men.

He pulled her tight against him. His arousal pulsed against her stomach, and she writhed against it, shaken when she realized he was as much a slave to their attraction as she was. Her arms went up and around his neck. His hands cupped her ass, moving her even more intimately against his excitement.

There was nothing beyond how good his mouth felt on hers, how her skin tingled everywhere it touched his. She needed more. He must have been feeling the same way because he yanked her skirt upward and slid his hands beneath the silk panties she'd impulsively worn beneath it. She frantically began to pull the front of his shirt out of his pants.

The sound of a knock on the door of his office brought Willa back to her senses. She pulled away from him and yanked her skirt down over her ass just in time to turn and face a very embarrassed secretary who stuttered her way through an apology before closing the door.

In a deep, gravelly voice, Lance asked, "What do we do about that, Willa?"

Nothing. I can't do this again. I can't open myself to that kind of pain a second time. Willa backed toward the door, grabbing her purse on the way. "Nothing. If you care about me at all—do nothing."

She was out the door and standing on shaking legs in the elevator before he had a chance to stop her. She brought a hand to her lips, lips still warm from his kiss. He raced after her and arrived just in time for the doors to close. He called out her name. She closed her eyes and turned away.

Lust was like a powerful narcotic. It felt good, but if a person gave in to it, it also had the ability to destroy them.

By the time the elevator opened on the first floor, Willa had composed herself. She took her shame, her embarrassment, and stuffed it deep down in the box in her gut where she kept all the feelings she didn't want to face.

Many things were better denied.

What good would come from resenting her parents for dying? For hating her elderly aunt and uncle for not wanting to raise her and Lexi? Did it matter why Lexi had taken her place and gone on the date with Lance?

I don't want to be angry all the time.

I don't want to hate myself or anyone else.

Willa hailed a cab and climbed in. Lance stepped outside of his building. She told the driver to go and faced forward.

I'm sorry, Lance.

A flash of herself in her college's clinic, discussing possibly terminating her pregnancy cut through her. *Did I lose the baby because I considered an abortion?*

Was it punishment for not being brave enough to tell anyone?

Not Lance?

Not Lexi?

Willa burst into tears in the back of the cab.

"Lady, are you okay?" the driver asked.

Willa shook her head. She was as far from being okay as she'd ever been.

And this is why I can't look back. This is who I become when I do. She thought about Kenzi's words. "None of us are who we were back then. Give yourself a chance to get to know who he is now."

Sorry, Kenzi. I know he's not the boy I slept with that summer. He's a man now—a man with the power to rip away my façade of strength.

I don't want to go back to hating myself.

I can't risk that.

No matter how much I may want to.

STILL CATCHING HIS breath from his sprint down the stairs, Lance watched Willa leave in a cab and stood rooted to the sidewalk for a long time. He'd finally gotten his answers, but they came with even more questions. Willa hadn't sent Lexi. Nothing about their first time together had been a game to her.

Which makes me even more of a dick than I thought.

Perfect.

How could anything that felt as good as being with Willa also hurt like an elephant had just kicked him in the balls. He wanted to grab the next cab, chase her down, and—and then what?

Her words came back to him. "If you care about me at all—do nothing." What the fuck did that mean?

"Lance Barrington?" a man asked as he approached, extending his hand for a shake as though they were old friends. Lance didn't recognize the man standing next to him expectantly.

He turned his head from the man and back toward the street. Following Willa wasn't an option, but nor was letting things end the way they had. He answered absently, "Yes."

"I'm Emmitt Kalling." The man dropped his hand once it became clear the greeting wasn't going to get any warmer. "Dax Marshall said you were in need of my services."

Lance shook his head. "Sorry, who are you and what are you doing here?"

"I'm a freelance security specialist." He lowered his voice and folded his arms across his chest, his sleeves pulling up enough to expose his web of tattoos that ran up his arms. He was exactly the type of security Lance imagined Dax would need to employ. "We should talk about this in a less public place."

"Dax called you?" Lance asked, not actually caring what he was saying. His attention had already slid away from the man to Willa. He ran their last conversation over in his head again and again. He shouldn't have pushed for the truth right away. He should have given her time. His impatience was that of the twenty-year-old he'd been. *Grow the fuck up.*

This doesn't have to be a repeat of the first time.

It was apparent Emmitt was quickly losing patience and looked as if he was barely holding back what he really wanted to say. "Yes, Dax Marshall. He said you were looking for added security. You had some sort of breach in the office. I can assure you if that's the case I'll track down the problem and it won't happen again. But I do think we should take this meeting elsewhere."

"No," Lance answered flatly. He had always handled his own business. The last thing he needed was another brother thinking he needed guidance.

"No there was no breach?" Emmitt asked, still clearly fighting his annoyance.

"No, I don't need your services. Dax was wrong," Lance said shortly. In that moment he didn't give a shit about the woman who had passed herself off as his secretary. All he cared about was that Willa was hurting, and she had cut him out of her life—again.

Expelling a harsh breath, Emmitt grunted, "I flew up from Texas because I was told you had a situation on your hands."

"I do," Lance said with a self-deprecating smile. "But it's nothing you can help me with." With that, Lance walked away from a very pissed-off-looking Emmitt. Normally he wouldn't have treated anyone that way, but he was irritated Dax had gone against his wishes. *And* he was at a loss for what his next step should be with Willa.

In the past he'd chosen to withdraw from the politics of his family and steer clear of emotionally messy situations. He'd been raised to keep his head down, his thoughts to himself, and to put peace within the family above his personal needs.

That was about to change.

He strode to the elevator and punched the button to his floor. He was still glowering as he walked through his secretary's office. She went three shades of red.

"I'm so sorry. I never would have. Please don't report this to the temp agency. I'm paying for college on this salary. God, I'm so sorry."

Lance waved a hand dismissively. "I'm not going to say anything." The last thing he needed was something else to feel badly about. His tie was suddenly too tight. He loosened it. "Am I a complete asshole?" he demanded.

With huge round eyes, the young woman answered, "I'm not qualified to answer that question, sir."

Lance paced in front of her desk. "She said the best thing I could do was leave her alone. You're a woman. Did she look like she meant it?"

The woman made a pained face and looked down at her desk.

"I left her alone the last time she asked me to. It made things worse. This time I'm handling it my way." A euphoric thought accompanied his decision. *God, she'd tasted so damn good.* If she'd felt nothing toward him, she would have never kissed him the way she had. No, she was holding back for some reason, and he intended to find out why.

In a weak voice, his secretary said, "If you don't tell me, I won't know anything if anyone asks."

Lance looked at her and realized she'd gone pale. He replayed his last words in his head and smiled wryly. "I'm not going to kidnap her." He arched an eyebrow. "Unless you think that would work."

The woman accidentally knocked her keyboard off her desk, bent to retrieve it, and looked sweaty and nervous when she met his eyes again. Her mouth opened and closed a few times like a fish trying to catch its breath.

I should probably tell her I'm kidding before she faints or calls the police. "How about you just order an insanely large bouquet and send it to this address." He wrote Willa's address on a sticky note. "In fact, have a bouquet sent there every day until I tell you to stop."

With that, Lance returned to his office. He answered several emails regarding the Capitol Complex project. Work always calmed him. It also gave him time to think before choosing his next step with Willa.

At half past eleven, he woke Clay with a phone call.

"Who is this?" Clay asked groggily.

"Lance."

"She's not here," he mumbled.

"Good. We need to be clear about something. Willa is mine. She can work for you if she wants to, but if you so much as flirt with her I will feed you your front teeth for lunch. I don't care if you're Dax's friend."

With just a hint of sarcasm, Clay said, "Got it. Don't fuck Willa. Anything else?"

Lance knew how to use a weakness, in buildings or people, to his benefit. If Clay was looking for a pet project, Lance could work with that. "I need to spend more time with her."

"Are you asking for my help?" Clay sounded pleased with the idea.

Better to have him working with me rather than against. Lance had gone over all the possible ways he could spend more time with Willa and this still made the most sense. "Yes. I want you to bring her with you when you meet with me."

Clay laughed. "I've never played matchmaker. Sounds fun." In a much more serious tone, as if he had just thought of something important, Clay asked, "What are your intentions?"

"My intentions?" Lance asked in disbelief.

"I'm not setting the two of you up for anything less than the real deal." He made a contemplative sound. "I feel responsible for her. She's my first personal assistant."

How is this ridiculous man Dax's best friend?

"Just bring her with you later today."

Lance hung up and stood. *What the hell am I doing?*

What I should have done a long time ago.

A thought occurred to him, and he buzzed through to his secretary. "Did you already send out the bouquet?"

"Yes, sir."

Shit. "I forgot to tell you what to write on the card."

"I improvised."

"What did you say?" *Do I want to know?*

She cleared her throat nervously. "I'm here when you're ready—Lance."

"I guess that's better than—I'm done being patient, it's time to fucking forgive me."

There was a light feminine laugh. "I thought so."

"What's your name?"

"Miss Oliviera."

"Miss Oliviera, when my regular secretary comes back,

apply for a position in my office. We'll find something for you."

"Thank you, sir." After a moment, she added, "I still won't lie to the police for you."

Lance laughed without humor and hung up. Hopefully it wouldn't come to that.

Chapter Eight

THREE MINUTES BEFORE noon, Willa stood next to the desk of Kate, Dax's secretary. "I'm meeting Mr. Landon. He's using an office here." She smiled apologetically. "I tried to call and confirm the location but . . ."

Kate smiled back in understanding. "Mr. Landon lives by his own schedule. Is today your first day?"

Willa nodded and adjusted her suit jacket. After leaving Lance's office that morning she'd gone for a long walk. Despite how her feet protested the high-heeled abuse, she felt calmer. Now that she knew her feelings for him were still there, bubbling below the surface, she would make sure she didn't put herself in a vulnerable position again. All she needed was distance for things to get back on track, to keep the past contained. "Do you know which office we'll be using?"

Kate referenced a notepad beside her computer. "Looks like the one right next to Mr. Marshall's."

Only because Kate was so easy to talk to, Willa said, "I get the feeling he wants to keep an eye on us."

Amusement twinkled in Kate's eyes. "He's becoming

quite the family man."

Family. Until recently Willa would have said hers consisted of only Lexi and Kenzi. When Kenzi married Dax, and there was no doubt that it would happen, it would make him a brother of sorts. "I've never had a big brother watching out for me."

"Not even all those Barringtons?"

Willa shrugged. *It hadn't been like that.* Kenzi used to avoid her family as much as possible, so Lexi and Willa had also. Even after moving to Boston to be closer to Kenzi, actual interaction with her family had been minimal. That had changed this past year after she met Dax. Kenzi was doing more and more with her family. It was good for Kenzi, but it did make things uncomfortable sometimes for Willa. None of that was appropriate to share with Dax's secretary, so Willa didn't.

"I suppose I should go see what the office looks like," Willa said.

Kate snapped her fingers and stood. "I can't believe I forgot about it. A box came this morning with your name on it."

"Mine? Really?"

They walked together to the office beside Dax's. On the desk there was indeed a huge wrapped box with Willa's name on it. Willa turned to ask Kate for a pair of scissors to open it and discovered that the other woman already had a pair with her. "I figured you might not have one yet."

There was a card taped to the outside of the box. Willa tore it open. In beautiful cursive writing it said, "Congratulations on your new job! Sophie and Dale."

Willa read it aloud, trying to hide her surprise, then added, "Kenzi's parents."

"That is so sweet," Kate cooed. "What do you think they sent? Do you mind if I stay and see?"

"Of course not," Willa said. Kenzi had said her relationship with her mother had become much closer recently. Was this an olive branch? A sign that Kenzi's parents wanted to get to know Kenzi's friends better as well? Strange, but after all the time she and Lexi spent with Kenzi, she didn't feel she really knew Kenzi's parents at all. She and Lexi had interacted with them as little as possible for Kenzi's sake. The idea was disconcerting.

Willa didn't let herself think about how much she missed her own mother. That sorrow was also buried deep within her. She cut the ribbon that held the box closed and ripped the paper away. As Willa took out each item she said the name of it slowly. In all her life she'd never received such a thoughtful gift. "There's a personalized desk calendar, stapler, letter opener. There's even a lunch bag with my name on it."

Kate clapped her hands together happily. "It's like school supplies you get every year when you start in a new class, isn't it?"

"I guess," Willa said after lining up the items on the desk. "My parents passed away when I was young. We lived at boarding school after that. The school supplied everything. We didn't get things like this."

"That's so sad," Kate said sincerely.

Willa shrugged. *Only if I remember. And I don't want to.* "Not really. It's just the way it was."

"Moving in?" Clay asked from the doorway.

Kate made a quick departure. Willa moved the box off the desk and hastily organized some of the items into the drawers of the desk. She paused when she realized he was watching her. *Oh, shit. This is his desk, really. And here I am putting stuff in the drawers like it's mine.* She started taking the items back out. "I'm sorry. This was delivered. I should have asked if you wanted any of it in your desk."

Clay leaned against the door jam. "Put whatever you want in here. Consider the office yours. I don't really do desks." He walked over and looked into the box on the floor. "Is that a lunch bag with your name on it?"

Willa blushed and pushed the box aside with her foot. "Sophie Barrington sent it. She must have heard I took this job." She took a deep breath and fought for inner calm. Seeing Lance that morning had brought everything back. Dark thoughts that had been securely tucked away were fighting for space in her head again. She was keeping it all contained, but it was taking everything she had.

Clay sized Willa up from head to toe. "And she likes you. Interesting."

He's curious, that's all. All I have to do is convince him that there is nothing interesting and he'll move on to something else. "I've known the family for a long time."

"The Barringtons are an intense bunch, aren't they? Really uptight."

Willa looked away, not wanting to say anything one way

or the other. She picked up the stapler to place it off to one side of the desk. "Every family has their good points and their challenges."

"Why didn't it work out between you and Lance?"

The stapler hit the floor. Willa scrambled to pick it up. She looked straight into Clay's eyes and lied. "There was never anything between us."

"You're not a good liar."

I can't do this. I won't do this. Willa straightened her shoulders. "Do you have a list of job responsibilities for me?"

Clay smiled. "I like you, Willa. You've got this genuine vibe going. I respect that. I get that none of this is my business, but it's like a car crash I can't look away from. What is it about Lance you don't like?"

Willa blushed again and hated that she wasn't better at hiding how she felt. Lexi would never betray herself that way.

Clay straightened from the door. "You *do* like him. Oh, that's even more interesting."

If Clay hadn't been blocking the only exit, Willa would have withdrawn. Feeling trapped, she forced a smile. "Like I said, I've known the family a long time. I like all of them."

Clay tapped a finger on his chin as he studied her. "You lie like someone who hates to, but you're willing to about this. Which means you're hiding something. Sweet Willa has a secret. That's it, isn't it? There's something you don't want anyone to know."

Willa's knees buckled beneath her, and she put a hand on the top of the desk to steady herself. There was only one way out of the situation outside of shoving him aside, and that was to convince him he was wrong. Willa straightened. "With that imagination you should write mysteries. There is no big secret. I'm not hiding anything. Now, if it's okay with you, I'd like get started on what you hired me for."

"Great, let's move this meeting over to Lance's office. He said he has some preliminary sketches he wants me to look over. You could take notes on what we discuss."

Bringing a shaky hand up to her mouth, Willa said, "I—I—"

Clay smiled again. "You don't want to go there."

Willa hugged her other arm to her stomach. "I don't want to go there."

"Because he slept with your twin?"

"No."

Snapping a finger in the air, Clay said, "He said he wanted to?"

Oh, my God. How do I stop this? "Mr. Landon. None of this is any of your business."

Clay rubbed his chin again. "I feel like I'm close. I don't believe there was nothing between you. Is he a sick bastard? Does he want to wear nylons during sex or something like that? I knew a guy like that once. Well, I knew his ex-girlfriend. She told me about it." He shuddered. "Try to get that image out of your head. I haven't been able to."

Willa blinked a few times then shook her head. *I have to get out of here.* She picked up her purse. "I really want to work for you, but this whole conversation is inappropriate." She looked pointedly at the door, hoping he'd get the hint and step aside.

In a much more serious tone, Clay asked, "Did he hurt you?"

Willa froze. She opened her mouth to say he didn't but no sound came out.

All amusement left Clay's expression. "He did hurt you."

"It was a very long time ago."

Clay folded his arms over his chest. "I don't think I want you seeing him."

There was an absurdity to the conversation that put a sad smile on Willa's face. "As I said it's not any of your business."

"A woman like you deserves someone nice."

"Like me?" For some reason his words struck a chord with her. The overwhelming memories she'd been pushing aside since she'd seen Lance that morning came rushing back. She thought about how she'd all but thrown herself at Lance the night they'd been together, how she hadn't told him about the pregnancy after she knew. She thought about how close she'd come to aborting the baby and how she'd lost it anyway after she'd decided to keep it. She'd been so angry after it happened that she'd slept with a few men she didn't care about just because she wanted to wipe Lance out of her mind. All that had done was make her feel worse. "You don't know me." Tears filled her eyes as she said the words.

"What the hell is going on in here?" Dax's voice boomed into the office, making Willa's humiliation complete.

"She's not crying because of me. Okay, partly because of me, but mostly because of your future brother-in-law Lance."

"Fuck," Dax said, pushing past Clay and closing the door behind him. He came to a stop a foot from Willa. "What did he do?"

"Nothing," Willa said, trying to blink away her tears.

"He did something," Clay said with authority. "But she won't tell me what."

Dax glared at his friend. "You couldn't stay out of my family, could you? You had to dig and dig until you found something. What am I supposed to do with this?"

Willa started to edge her way out of the office. "Nothing. This is just a big misunderstanding."

Dax took out his phone. "I'm calling Kenzi."

"No," Willa said and grabbed his phone. "Don't. Please don't." Dax and Clay looked at her as if she was losing her mind. Willa held his phone to her chest. "There is nothing to tell her because nothing happened."

There was a cold anger in Dax's eyes that sent a shiver down Willa's spine. "Willa, if he hurt you in any way . . ."

Willa closed her eyes briefly as the enormity of where this was going sunk in. Kenzi had just confessed to her family that she'd been raped as a teenager. Dax was the first person Kenzi had told. He was looking at this situation through that lens. "It's not what you're thinking, Dax."

Dax stepped closer to her. "Did. He. Hurt. You?"

A tear spilled down Willa's cheek even as she lied. "No."

In a gentle tone Dax said, "Don't protect him, Willa. And don't be afraid. No one will think any less of you."

Angrily wiping her tears away, Willa said, "Why are you doing this?" More tears spilled over. "I need to get out of here." She handed his phone back to him and pushed past both of them.

Dax stepped in front of her. "Kenzi thought the truth would turn people away from her, but it didn't. If something happened, even with her brother, she could help you."

"Please let me leave."

Dax folded his arms across his chest. "I will if you can look me in the eye and tell me that Lance didn't hurt you."

It was too much. Too emotional. Too confusing. Willa said more than she meant to. "He didn't mean to. We were young. He'd been drinking when I went to see him..." Willa's voice trailed away as she realized that the way she'd said it fit with what Dax thought. "It isn't what you think."

Dax seemed to grow taller with anger. He turned to Clay. "Where is Lance now?"

"At his office, I imagine. We had planned to meet him there," Clay said.

Turning on his heel, Dax strode out of the office.

Willa stood in frozen horror, then bolted after him. "Don't do this, Dax."

Dax shook his head. "Lance needs to know he can't—"

"If you do this, the only one you'll hurt is me," Willa implored, putting up her hand to stop him.

Kate discretely left her office. Clay came to stand beside Willa.

I've kept it secret this long. Please, help me find the words to stop this. "I know you care about me, Dax. But you need to respect me, too. I'm asking you to stay out of it." She turned pleading eyes to Clay. "You, too. This is a game to you, but it's my life. Please."

Clay grimaced. "It was a game at first, but not now. Now I feel like an ass."

With anger still burning in his eyes, Dax said, "If he hurts you again, I'll kill him. Even if he is Kenzi's brother."

"It wasn't what you think, Dax. Lance would never do that. I can't say more than that." Willa let out a shaky breath. "Please keep this between us."

A curt nod was Dax's concession.

Tears of gratitude poured down Willa's cheeks. Dax pulled her to his chest and gave her a brotherly hug. When Willa composed herself, he handed her a tissue from Kate's desk.

Clay held out his arms, but Willa didn't step into them. He made a face at her. "Really? Oh, I see how it is. I'll keep your damn secret, too, but that hurt."

Willa shook her head ruefully then hugged him. There was no attraction, no zing with Clay, and the hug was just as non-sexual as Dax's had been. The man had layers. *Who knew?*

Over her head he asked, "I've always wanted a little sister. Can I have her?"

Willa stepped out of his arms. His comment made her smile even though her emotions were still all over the place. "It doesn't work that way."

Dax looked relieved that the emotional storm had passed. He joked to Clay, "We'll share her."

There was a knock on the outside door of the office. Kate popped her head in. "Mr. Barrington's secretary called and would like to know what time to expect Mr. Landon this afternoon."

Clay waved a hand in her direction. "I'm not able to make the meeting. My schedule is booked."

Willa swallowed and shot Clay a grateful look.

Kate looked back and forth at the people in the room. "Do you want me to call—?"

Dax shook his head curtly. "We're all set."

Kate ducked back out and closed the door behind her.

The room was awkwardly quiet for a long moment. Willa cleared her throat and said, "Thank you."

Clay arched an eyebrow. "If that's all settled, can we move along to *my* problem?"

Dax rolled his eyes skyward as if asking for strength. "And that is?"

"What the hell does a personal assistant do?" Clay asked with a straight face, then he smiled. "'Cause I have no fucking idea."

Willa found herself smiling along with him. "I don't either."

A corner of Dax's mouth twitched as if he were amused but not giving in to it. "Willa is not working for you, Clay. She'll work here. Willa, ask Kate what she needs help with."

Yes, Dax was still talking about her as if she couldn't make decisions for herself, but now that Willa knew he genuinely did care about her, she could forgive his Neanderthal side. Somehow it made her feel safe the way she had when her parents had been alive. She'd thought she wanted to escape the situation in Boston, but no matter where she went, the past would still be there.

It had been a very long day and the idea of working with Kate was a welcome one. Willa didn't want to play twenty questions every day with a boss who didn't actually need an employee.

Her next question was an awkward one to ask, but she'd promised Lexi she would help with the bills. Whether they continued to live together or if she moved out, Willa still needed a job that would support her. "Will I still get paid?"

Clay nodded authoritatively. "Absolutely. In fact, I believe your salary should be doubled. Isn't that right, Dax?" He quoted a monthly amount that was equal to what had once been Willa's annual salary.

Dax shot Clay a skeptical look. "For an assistant to my secretary?"

"Little sisters are expensive." Clay shrugged. "She could always still work for me."

Dax pinned Willa down with a serious look. "Don't say a word to Kate about your salary."

"I won't," Willa promised. "But you don't need to pay me that much. I'm okay with whatever the regular rate for someone in that position would be."

Clay smiled proudly. "Isn't she the cutest?" His expression darkened. "I still want to punch Lance."

"You can't," Willa interjected quickly. If there was one sure-fire way of bringing the past into the forefront, that would be it.

"He won't," Dax said in a tone that delivered a warning to his friend as well.

That evening, Lance parked his car outside the proposed Capitol Complex site. He found a bench near it and watched people move through the area in front of it and between the side buildings. His head was churning with questions. He visually calculated the space, cataloguing permanent structures as well as those that could be removed to improve the flow. It calmed him. He did his clearest thinking when he distracted himself with mathematics. Things that appeared random made sense. Events could be predicted.

Some architects were artists. They envisioned something and then sought practical methods to make them possible. Lance started with a solid foundation and worked his way up. He was often brought in on projects as the voice of reason. Some called him the Dream Crusher.

His office building had been his sole creation and represented his preferred style. Its structural strength, though, and how he'd designed the building to be able to withstand almost anything in nature, hadn't impressed Willa. She'd said it lacked warmth, which from a business point of view had never been important to him. His buildings were in demand because they were brilliantly designed.

But they don't connect with people enough that they want to return to them?

Is that how she sees me?

Clay had canceled their meeting without explanation. If the reason had been Clay's, Lance was reasonably certain he would have told him. Even if only to stir up trouble. The excuse about being too busy was bullshit.

Why would Clay bother with an excuse?

Did Willa say she didn't want to see me?

Is she with him now?

His phone rang. He checked the caller ID. *Ian. Shit. Thursday. I forgot about family game night.* He let it go through to his voice service.

He checked through his text messages. There was nothing from Willa.

He rummaged through his computer bag for a moment and pulled out the leather journal he'd intended to give her that morning. His aunt had never done anything for his family while she was alive; it made sense that her journal wouldn't either.

He opened the top cover and the black card fell onto his lap. He turned it between his fingers. The woman who'd left the card had expressed disappointment in his lack of curiosity. His team didn't know who she was, but he should find out. Historically, at least where family shit was concerned, the Barringtons didn't ask questions. Personal topics were minefields that were best avoided completely.

He used to agree with that philosophy, but that was a roadblock that had stopped him from forcing the truth out of Willa earlier. *I would have done so many things differently had I known Lexi was the reason for the switch. I would have never called her immature or dismissed what she felt for me. I thought it was a childish prank and my pride had been hurt.*

I should have made the truth a priority. My body knew it wasn't her that day, I should have known that Willa wouldn't have lied to me.

A part of me knew, but pushing Willa for answers risked

bringing the wrath of my family down on me and I hadn't been willing to do that back then.

Because peace must be maintained.

Fuck peace.

He turned to the page of the journal and began to read with a somewhat defiant interest. *If there is something here I'll find it.* By the time he was halfway through the entries he was certain of one thing—the planet was better off without his aunt. The pages overflowed with bitterness, paranoia, and cold decisions to make people pay for betraying her. Strings of numbers, possibly phone numbers, were written with no explanation in the margins. None of it was written in the linear fashion of a sane person. Some numbers appeared scattered, seeming to start on one page and continue on another. There were also several references to his mother being pregnant with twins, then pages had been torn out. He now saw why Emily had wanted to ask his mother about her sister. The animosity his aunt had had for his mother was disturbing. Had that played a role in his mother's breakdown?

Two nine seven. Was it an area code? He looked it up on his smartphone. It was the country code for the island of Aruba. That was where Kenzi was born. And Kent, her twin, who had died. He read the entries before the torn-out pages again then the ones that followed.

His aunt might have needed phone numbers in Aruba to call and see how Sophie was. After all, his mother had been admitted to the hospital for almost a week when Kenzi and Kent had been premature.

Patrice didn't sound like someone who would call to comfort her sister.

Lance read the entire journal again, this time earmarking pages that referenced his family. When the streetlights came on and it became difficult to read, Lance closed the book, returned it to his computer bag, and got back into his car. He'd have someone look into those numbers. They were probably nothing, but he couldn't shelve the journal until he knew for sure. No, he didn't have the type of security Dax and Asher required, but he had people.

He drove home, stripped, and took a quick shower before flopping on his bed in his lounge pants. Only because he couldn't not do it, he texted Willa.

I'm sorry I upset you.

When there was no immediate answer, he tossed the phone onto the bed beside him. She'd asked him to stay away, but he couldn't. He had to know she was okay.

His phone beeped to announce a new message. *Willa.* **I'm sorry, too. I shouldn't have left the way I did.**

He answered, **I'm not sorry I kissed you.**

Silence.

He added, **I can't pretend I don't want you. That's how I know the difference between you and your sister. You're the one who reduces me to a bumbling idiot.**

Her answer tore at his heart. **I can't do this. I got your flowers. Don't wait for me, Lance. I won't change my mind.**

He sighed. If she hadn't kissed him the way she had, he would have been able to accept the finality of her words. She'd clung to him like a returning lover who'd built up a hunger as deep as his for her. There had to be a way to reach her. He almost texted her again, but instead called her.

"Lance—" she said in a panicked voice.

"Willa, don't hang up. When I look back I see a hundred ways I screwed up with you. The biggest mistake I made was rushing you. I hurt you, and I can't change that. I can promise it'll be different this time. If you give us a chance, we'll go as slowly as you want to."

"I can't . . ."

"Tell me what you need, Willa, and we'll start there."

For a long moment all he heard was her shaky breathing. "I want to be happy, Lance. I don't know if I can do that if I open a door to the past."

"Then we start fresh today."

"You say that like it's possible."

"Anything is possible, Willa, if you want it enough. Do you? Want this?"

He held his breath.

"Yes," she said softly. "And no. Oh, God, I don't know. It's been a long day. I can't think."

If he were beside her, his arms would be around her. He used what calmed him to reassure her. "When I start a new project, I don't design it in one day. I know what I want to build, but creating it takes time. I focus on one element before addressing the next. In the end, my structures surpass safety standards. In earthquakes, other buildings fall, but mine stand. The strength is in the details."

"And what do you want to build with me?" Willa asked just above a whisper.

"If you're asking me where this will go, Willa, I don't know. What I do know is, whatever we have is too damn real to walk away from. That's where I want to start. I simply want to be with you."

"I don't know, Lance. There's so much—"

"There isn't, Willa, because I met you for the first time today. Remember? I was the hot guy you bumped into on the street. We took one look at each other, and it was instant lust. I kissed you. I couldn't help myself. You slapped me and told me I was out of line."

Lance was rewarded with a chuckle. "You're crazy."

"I sent you flowers. You spent the day thinking about how gorgeous I am . . ."

"In my fantasy you're a little more humble."

"Your fantasy." Lance sighed. *Finally.* "Tell me your version."

After a quiet moment, Willa said, "We met on the street next to the capitol building. I didn't know you were the one who had been awarded the contract. You asked me what I thought about the project. I said something that you found so amazing you wrote it down. You said something that made me laugh. We found a coffee shop and talked until it closed . . ." Her voice trailed away.

"What time?" he asked.

"I'm sorry?"

"What time do you want to meet at the capitol building? I'll bring a notebook and polish my joke-telling skills."

"I have a job now."

With Clay. Lance held his tongue. Willa was close to saying yes. "I'll be on a bench in front of the building at six. Come meet me for the first time, Willa." He hung up because he had a feeling she needed time before she decided.

Chapter Nine

>>>>><<<<<

AT FIVE FIFTY-FIVE, Willa stepped out of a cab and froze just before turning onto the street where Lance said he would be sitting, waiting for her. She leaned back against the cornerstone of a building and took several calming breaths.

Will he be there?

And, if he is, can we really move forward without looking back?

Am I a fool to think it's possible?

The memory of how good his mouth felt on hers, how much pleasure merely being in his presence brought her, surged through her, but was it worth the risk?

It wasn't that she was lonely, but that only one man had ever made her feel scandalously impulsive. That man was waiting for her a few hundred feet away. As soon as she stepped from behind the building, she was agreeing to give him a second chance.

"Are you okay?" a beautiful, tall, brunette with more piercings and tattoos than clothing asked.

Willa straightened off the building. "Yes. No." She chuckled with self-deprecation. "I'm not really sure."

"You need help?"

Since the other woman probably thought Willa was crazy, Willa didn't see that she had much to lose by confirming her first impression. "Could you see if there is a man with dark brown hair sitting on a bench just round the corner?"

With an amused expression, the woman stepped away from the building and peered down the street. "There is, and he's looking around for someone." The woman smiled and waved. "Yes, I'm waving at you, Mr. Hunk-in-a-Suit. He doesn't know what to do. How adorable. He just looked away. He's still looking around. Yep, I'm still here waving at you, Mr. Hot Stuff." The woman laughed. "He just gave me the *I'm not interested* cold shoulder. Is he waiting for you?"

If Willa hadn't been an internal nervous wreck she would have laughed at the playful way the woman had handled the odd request. "Yes."

The woman gave Willa a long once-over then sized up Lance again. "Is he a cop?"

"No, he's an architect."

"So why are you hiding?"

Because I'm a coward. Willa straightened her shoulders and adjusted her purse beneath her arm. *Correction, I was a coward. Life is about moving forward and growing. If I stay here, or worse turn and leave, what does it say about who I am? I will never be more than the devastated girl I once was. I will have allowed one event to define me.* "I'm not," Willa said firmly and stepped from behind the building. "Not anymore."

Lance stood as soon as he saw her and the smile on his

face brought an answering one to Willa's. They met halfway and stood for a long moment simply staring into each other's eyes. Willa broke the silence first. "I hear this whole area will be renovated soon; at least that's what the papers say."

"I heard the same. A project like that could have a large impact on the community."

Without looking away from Lance's near-black, beautiful eyes, Willa said breathlessly, "There's so much history here already. I hope they don't change it as much as they celebrate it. It's a place where people can and should be heard, but also where they could gather to hear music. I'd love to see the side road closed off and the parking lot made into a park with trees."

"I'd write that down, but I doubt I'll forget a word you say to me today," Lance said with such intensity that Willa believed him. He held out his hand in greeting as if they were meeting for the first time. "My name is Lance."

Willa shook his hand, loving how his enveloped hers. "Willa."

"Will-ah you go for coffee with me?" Lance asked with a straight face.

It took a moment for the joke to sink in but when it did Willa laughed and shook her head. "You had all night to come up with a joke and that's what you chose?" She was smiling, though.

He turned and tucked her hand into the crook of his arm, and they started walking together down the street. "I hoped it would make you smile, and it did."

Willa laughed again. How could being with Lance feel

so . . . right? *Because this is today, not yesterday. And we're starting again.* Being with Lance felt right. They strolled to a café and chose an outside table. Lance held out a chair for her then took the one across from her. They ordered sandwiches and lattes that arrived almost instantly.

"How was work?" Lance asked after they'd both dug into their food and exhausted all safe topics like the temperate weather that evening and the quality of the waitstaff.

"Better than my first day," Willa answered honestly. She still couldn't believe she and Lance were out on a date. "I never pictured myself working in an office, but it'll pay the bills, and I'm grateful for the opportunity."

"Did Clay take the office in Dax's building?" Lance asked before taking another bite of his sandwich.

For a moment, Willa debated exactly how much to say. This was a fresh start, and she wanted it to be an honest one. "No. It didn't work out with Clay. He didn't really have a need for a personal assistant. I'm working with Kate instead. Filing. Typing. Things like that."

"I'm sorry it—" Lance smiled sheepishly. "I'm not actually sorry. That wasn't the job for you, Willa. The one for Dax isn't either, though. You've always loved art. You should ask Emily if she knows of something. Her museum is doing well."

Willa nodded. "And she has that whole school she and Asher are building in New Hampshire."

"You wouldn't want to live in New Hampshire," Lance said confidently.

Willa sat back in her chair. "Really? And why is that?"

He winked. "I'm in Boston."

With more amusement than sarcasm, Willa asked, "Are Barrington boys born with enormous egos or do they develop over time?"

Neither Lance nor Willa could stop smiling. He wiggled his eyebrows at her. "I could say what we're born with that *is* impressively large, but I'm on first-date best behavior."

Willa burst out laughing then bent forward, embarrassed she'd laughed so loudly. "What would your mother think of a comment like that?"

Covering his heart with his hand, Lance laughed right along with her. "She'd be mortified. Dad would give me that disappointed look of his. You know the one."

"Where his eyebrows try to meet in the middle and you can actually count the lines on his forehead?"

"Two lines and you're safe. Four and there is no escaping the lecture."

"I never thought of it that way, but you're right. Oh my God, now I won't be able to keep a straight face if he does it. I'm in trouble."

Lance reached over and took her hand in his. "We can be in trouble together." His action and comment surprised both of them. They both froze.

Willa's heart started beating wildly. It was good, but it was also too good, too soon. She felt panic closing in.

Lance seemed to sense her reaction and said, "Like the time Andrew took Asher's Lamborghini for a joy ride."

Willa remembered the story. "So Asher took your father's and hunted him down."

"Both cars came back with dents. Dad was so angry, but he wouldn't say it because he didn't want to upset Mom."

Willa saw a flash of something in Lance's eyes, and she understood why. As funny as the memory was, it also highlighted Sophie's fragile mental state. Willa gave Lance's hand a gentle squeeze.

Lance turned Willa's hand over in his, tracing her wrist with his thumb. That simple act was enough to send flutters of need through Willa. Her eyes flew to his lips then up to meet his heated gaze. She could almost feel his mouth trailing kisses down her neck, his tongue circling her nipples. She didn't want to hold his hand, she wanted to feel it gripping her ass, sliding around to caress her sex. Her mouth parted as she imagined his strong fingers wet from her juices, thrusting up into her. *Oh, yes.* All that, from just his thumb caressing her wrist.

His eyes burned with a passion that flamed hers. "God, I want to fuck you."

Yes.

He closed his eyes and pinched the bridge of his nose with the hand that had held hers. "I shouldn't have said that."

Right. Bad idea. Remember that, Willa.

Willa fought to bring her breathing back to normal and didn't agree or disagree. This part of their relationship had never wavered. It might have been denied, but it was as strong now as it had been when they were younger. *I want him, too. If I'm honest about that, will it balance the score card? I never told him what happened. Is saying nothing lying?*

Can we do this? Can we choose our own reality as long as it's one we both agree on?

Why is being with Lance as terrifying as it is good?

Because this time, Lexi isn't messing it up. Lance's level of interest in me isn't in question.

It's all on me.

And if I can hold my shit together enough to let myself have this.

I'M A FUCKING idiot. I finally get Willa on a date and all I can talk about is the size of my dick and how much I want to do her.

Brilliant.

Well, played.

Fuck.

Willa was looking like if she could think of an excuse to flee from him she would. He didn't blame her. He wasn't a hormone-crazed teenager anymore. He dated women on a regular basis, but none of them could shut down his brain with a single look.

He'd promised her they'd take it slowly. He'd spent the night charting out how that would likely manifest. He'd been prepared to drop her off at her place, kiss her briefly, and walk away.

He needed to rethink that plan.

He didn't trust himself alone with her.

Whenever their eyes met, the attraction they shared sizzled. It wasn't that he thought she would turn him down. He imagined having her half undressed before the elevator made it to the floor of her apartment. He could have her panties gone and be joyfully, intimately tasting her before they made it a foot in the door. He would use everything he learned about pleasing a woman and see what sent her out of control. Her pleasure would be his. Again and again until he finally fucked her against the wall, or the couch . . . whatever was closest. He knew she would welcome him inside her as she had before. Only this time, she'd be calling out in orgasm as he pounded into her. He wouldn't come until she had more than once.

And then?

He remembered how she'd looked tucked against him, declaring that she loved him. His gut clenched with guilt. He'd hurt her once. And given how she had bolted from his office yesterday, she wasn't over it. Yes, they had begun the process of clearing the air, but they had a long way to go. This wasn't just any woman. This was Willa. She had always held a precious part of his heart. Her gentleness, her sincerity, her loveliness.

I won't hurt her again.

This wasn't about having her body. He wanted all of her.

That would take self-control.

In a strangled voice, he asked, "Are you working tomorrow?"

She looked as confused as he felt. "What is tomorrow? Saturday? No."

He took her hand in his again. "Spend the day with me."

Her mouth parted, and her tongue wet her bottom lip in the most delicious way. "What do you have in mind?"

"I don't know yet." *Because I have no fucking idea what we can do that will keep my hands off you, but I'll find something.*

She looked uncertain. "What should I wear?"

His dick throbbed as a hundred suggestions came to mind that he dismissed as inappropriate. "Something casual. Jeans. It's the season for outdoor art festivals. I'll see what's around. We can start at the south end then find someplace for dinner. Maybe walk around Faneuil Hall afterward."

A huge smile spread across her face. "Sounds perfect."

Perfect? Maybe not, but safer than anything else I could think of. "Have you been to Emily's museum?"

"Yes, but only briefly with Kenzi." Willa's blonde curls shone beneath the café's lighting that turned on as the sun set, giving her an angelic glow. "I don't fangirl over much, but I am in awe of her. And her mother? I wish I could have met her. Have you experienced her works? I thought I understood what three-dimensional art was until I touched hers. Somehow she captured the essence of moments in time. That's the only way I can describe it. You don't know what the piece is about, and then, suddenly you do. It rips through you, pulls an emotional response out of you, and leaves you different than before you touched it. Better somehow. Emily has the same gift." She stopped, looking self-conscious. "Sorry. I guess I have a strong opinion."

"And I have somewhere to take you on Sunday. If you'd like, I'll ask Emily to give us a private tour. She loves that." *Two dates. Say yes, Willa.*

"She offered one to me, but she's so pregnant I declined."

"I'll see how she feels. She really does enjoy explaining the process and telling the story behind each work. It would be good for me to hear some of it again. I'm looking for inspiration for the Capitol Complex. They accepted my initial proposal, but I want to add to it. It lacked—" He stopped. He almost said warmth, but he didn't want to spook her again. "Depth. You could help me rectify that."

Willa's eyes widened again as if he'd offered her a chance at something she wasn't ready to believe was possible. "I could try."

They fell into an awkward silence.

A man with a huge dog walked by. Lance chose a safe topic. "I never thought much about dogs, but my sister loves the one she adopted."

"Who wouldn't love Taffy? She's the biggest love bug. I watch her sometimes when she and Dax travel."

Lance remembered something Kenzi had said about Willa wanting to travel. "If you could go anywhere, where would that be?"

"You'll think I'm crazy."

"Tell me," he said. He wanted . . . no needed, to know what she yearned for.

"Disney."

"The theme park?"

Willa fiddled with the silverware beside her plate before answering. "Any part of it. My family used to talk about going when Lexi and I were young. We never made it there." She shrugged one of her delicate shoulders. "It's silly, really.

It'd probably make me sad now."

Okay, so no Disney. At least, not yet.

"Where else would you want to go?"

"I don't know. I haven't been many places." Willa looked painfully unsure of herself. "Most of the vacations Lexi and I took were either with your family or places we went together. And Lexi hates to fly. It's how our parents died."

He'd known that, but it was different hearing about it from her. It made it more real. It also explained the bond she had with Kenzi. When it came to family, he'd never heard of her having any outside of Lexi. "How about you?"

"Oddly, flying has never bothered me. I guess I figure that if something is going to go wrong it will—you don't have to leave the ground to crash and burn."

The way she said the last part made Lance wonder what he'd missed. He'd known her, at least from a distance, for a long time. Outside of her parents he wasn't aware of anything tragic happening to her. Apparently, he didn't know her as well as he thought he did.

That'll change. I want to know everything about her this time.

First, I'd be satisfied with simply seeing her smile again. He pointed to an elderly couple walking hand in hand by the café. "Do you ever look at people and try to guess their stories?"

Willa looked at the couple, then back at Lance. "All the time. I love things like that. I bet she was a ballet dancer. The elegant way she walks, her posture."

Lance nodded and added, "He had a boring life before someone dragged him to *Giselle*, and he saw her."

With a dreamy expression, Willa put her hand on Lance's arm as she watched the couple disappear down the street. "He bought tickets for every performance just to see her until he worked up the courage to ask her out."

"She said no because she was dating a man with no neck and the body of a linebacker."

"She changed her mind when he sent her a card with flowers and a poem about how beautifully she danced." Willa laughed and realized she was still holding Lance's arm. There was wonder in her eyes. "I didn't picture you as someone with an imagination." She looked instantly contrite. "I didn't mean that the way it sounded."

He caressed one of her cheeks lightly with the back of his fingers. "I can see why you'd think that. You only know me as the person I am around my family." He thought about how his life had become more and more structured, closing in until there wasn't much beyond who his family had wanted him to be. Asking Willa out was the first impulsive action he'd taken in a long time. "I like you, Willa Chambers. And I like who I am when I'm with you."

She nodded but didn't say anything. It was ironic in a way how their roles had reversed the second time around. She looked as scared by his declaration as he'd been by hers ten years earlier. To put her at ease he pointed to a mother and a daughter and asked her what she thought their story would be.

Their conversation fell into a comfortable pace and time

flew. A waitress apologized and said the café was closing. Lance paid the bill and handed her a generous tip.

With his hand on her lower back, Lance guided Willa out of the café and to the street. He hailed a cab and held the door open for her. "I'll pick you up tomorrow at ten."

She nodded and looked up at him, expecting the kiss he was dying to give her. He had watched her lips all evening. When she spoke, when she sipped her coffee, when she laughed. *So beautiful. Kissable.* Not his yet. *But almost.*

He bent until his lips hovered above hers. His breath mingled with hers. He could almost taste her but he wouldn't. Patience.

"See you tomorrow," Lance said and raised his head.

Willa blinked, shook her head, then ducked into the cab. "I'll be ready."

Lance shut the door and stepped back. This wasn't about ignoring an elder brother's mandate. He wanted Willa as much now as he had back then, but he was different. Her happiness was all that mattered.

I'm doing it right this time.

But that didn't make it easy.

Chapter Ten

>>>><<<<

WILLA WAS IN the bathroom of her apartment applying lipstick when Lexi appeared in the doorway behind her. "Whoa. Makeup. Hair down. You look awesome. What's the occasion?"

Beside her, Lexi ran a hand through her tangle of hair. When she did, it lifted the hem of her very short nightgown and revealed matching panties. *I'll meet Lance on the street.* "I didn't hear you come in last night."

"I hit the sack early. I was beat. You were out late, though. I almost called you. I was worried."

"Lex, I was fine." *Just shows how much I haven't been living life if she is worried about one late night. Not that I ever know where she is lately.* Normally Willa would feel sad by their lack of daily interaction, but that morning it actually worked to her advantage. Lance Barrington was not a topic she was ready to talk to Lexi about.

Lexi turned and half sat on the sink counter. "I hate it when we fight, Willa."

Meeting her sister's eyes, Willa smiled sadly, "Me, too."

"I should have told you the flash mob was for Lance. I

don't know what I was thinking. Well, actually, I do. I hate that I messed it up for the two of you the first time, and I know you still like him. I guess I thought that if me pretending to be you didn't work, then maybe you pretending to be me would. I know that's fucked up."

Willa closed her eyes briefly and gathered her scattering thoughts. Her mother's words from long ago came back to her after one of their sister-to-sister fights. *You'll only ever have one sister, one twin, Wil. Treasure her.* It didn't need to be perfect to be good. She opened her eyes and leaned over to hug Lexi. "It is, but it's also sweet in a way." She thought about the last heated argument she'd had with Lexi and added, "I never meant to make you feel badly about the way you live your life."

Lexi hugged her tightly. "Things were easier when we were younger. It was us against the world. What happened?"

Willa tensed and the hug ended. "Everyone grows up."

After another head-to-toe assessment of Willa, Lexi said, "There's something you're not telling me."

"Yes, there is," Willa said firmly. "And that's okay." She walked out of the bathroom and Lexi followed her.

"Since when do we have secrets?"

Since longer than you know, Willa thought sadly. There was a time when Lexi would have been the first person Willa would tell about something as big as spending the day with Lance. She didn't want the past to have a hold over the present, but in this situation it did. No matter how much she tried to tell herself that she trusted her sister, she couldn't trust her with this. *How do I make this okay?* "I'm going out for the day, and I don't really want to talk about it with you. I want this to be something that is mine. Just mine. Can you respect that?"

"Now you really have me worried. Tell me this isn't about Clay Landon."

That's an easy one. "It's not."

"But it's about a man, isn't it?"

Willa gave her sister a deliberately blank look.

Lexi waved her hand in frustration. "Sure. Why tell *me*? I'm only your twin sister."

With a sigh, Willa walked into the other room to find her phone and purse.

Lexi called out as she followed. "Just the one who shared a womb with you."

"We're not talking about this," Willa called back. Her phone beeped with a message. Lance asked her to meet him downstairs. *Thank God.* Hesitating at the door, Willa looked across the living room at her sister who was watching her leave. She hated the cavernous divide between them. "I need time to figure some things out before I can share them with you, but that doesn't mean I don't love and appreciate you, Lexi. That will never change." With that Willa walked out of their apartment and closed the door behind her.

Lance met her at the door of her building. For just a moment everything else fell away. The navy T-shirt he'd chosen complemented his muscular chest and arms. His jeans were worn enough so they were a frequent comfort choice. The suited, formal Lance she saw even at his parents' home was absent. It made Willa wonder, in a good way, if she knew him at all. He kissed her on the cheek in greeting, lingering briefly as if tempted to do more.

"Ready?" he asked, stepping back to look at her appreciatively.

"I am," she answered, her mouth dry from nerves.

"You look awesome."

"Thank you." She almost said he did, too, but she was more cautious this time.

He walked her to his hybrid sedan and opened the door for her. Willa glanced up at the window of her apartment and saw Lexi watching her. *Did I honestly think she wouldn't? Don't get involved, Lexi. I don't know if I could forgive you again. This time you were warned.* Their eyes met across the distance before Lexi let the curtain fall as she turned away.

Perhaps noticing an expression of distress on Willa's face, Lance asked, "Is everything all right?"

Willa turned and slid into the car. Her stomach was twisted in knots. *How am I going to look happy while trying not to throw up? I should have told Lexi where I was going. Did I just create a problem where there hadn't been one?*

For God's sake, can't I let myself simply be fucking happy? She forced a smile to her lips. "Wonderful. Let's get out of here."

Lance walked around the car and got into the driver's seat. Before starting it, he put his hands on the steering wheel and looked as if he were engaged in an inner debate. Finally, he glanced over at her. "Did you have breakfast?"

Not able to imagine eating anything while her stomach was churning the way it was, Willa said, "Yes."

He nodded. "Great. We'll head right to the NOWA open market. It's a craft and art fair."

Another surprise, or is he saying what he thinks I want to hear? There was nothing about his expression, however, that implied he was anything but happy about the idea. *Don't look for problems.* "Is this your first?"

He started the car and pulled out into the Boston traffic. "Art fair? No. I prefer them to galleries. More authentic. I have a few pieces hanging in my apartment from a relatively unknown artist, Simon Graft. And you never know who you'll meet. Three years ago I came across a man who painted landscapes with Caspar Friedrich's flair."

"I love his works. At first glance some seem dark and somber, but they draw you into their story."

Lance looked pleased that she understood. "Exactly. I bought one of Simon's paintings for my place, then went back and hired him to paint my mother's garden. My mother loved it so much she showed it to all of her friends. She knows everyone. His paintings are now in hotels all over the world."

His voice, his story . . . they washed everything else away. This side of him was unexpected and wonderful. "I sent your mother a bouquet of flowers with a thank you for the care package she gave me."

Lance smiled. "She'll love it." He navigated a busy intersection then glanced at Willa again. "I called Emily, and we're all set for a private tour with her tomorrow. She asked if we were going to join everyone for dinner at my parents' afterward. I didn't say yes, but I didn't say no either. I wanted to know how you felt about going there with me. On one hand it's early to 'take you home' so to speak, but on the other hand you already know everyone, and they'd love to see you."

Willa gripped the front of her seatbelt as if it were a lifeline. If they'd never hooked up. If the condom hadn't broken and she hadn't—

If we didn't have history, what would I say to an amazing man who liked me enough that he wanted his family to know we are together?

Wouldn't it be an easy yes?

It's not like we'll be able to hide what we're doing. Everyone will know soon enough.

She thought about her earlier conversation with Dax and cringed. *What will he think when he finds out? Will he say anything to Kenzi?*

Probably not, unless he thinks I need protecting, which is a good argument for simply letting everyone see us together.

"I'd love to have dinner with your family," Willa said with forced brightness. "Will Kenzi be there?"

"Probably. She's spending more time with our parents lately."

"That's really nice to hear," Willa said sincerely.

"It is," Lance agreed easily. "So, I'll tell them we'll be there?"

Willa swallowed hard. "Absolutely."

LANCE VALET PARKED at a hotel a street over from the park. As he and Willa walked toward the fair, he wondered if asking her to have dinner with his family had been a mistake. Things were going well. Part of him wanted to keep her to himself and ensure it stayed that way.

He wanted this time to be different, though, and that meant not hiding it from his family. This wasn't him breaking any rules and sneaking around with his little sister's best friend. He didn't need anyone's permission or approval, and dating her out in the open would make that clear without the necessity of actually saying it.

He didn't usually take his dates to his family, but Willa wasn't just a date. He didn't know what exactly they were, or would ever be to each other, but she was important to him.

He thought back to how badly things had gone the first time Kenzi brought Dax home and said the same thing about him. Asher and Ian had been the classic asses they often were. They wouldn't be like that to Willa, though. They already cared about her.

As they stepped onto the park grounds, he took Willa's hand in his, and it felt like the most natural thing to do. Yes, the attraction was still there and pulsing between them, but there was also an easiness with her. He didn't worry that she was after his money. She wasn't using him for his connections. He could be himself with her, the man he was with his closest friends.

The day went too fast. They strolled through the booths learning about each other as they explored all forms of artwork. They marveled at the creative possibilities of blown glass, then laughed as they challenged each other to find the most offensive T-shirt in the place.

They were still laughing over one when they ran into two of his close friends. Thomas was a corporate lawyer who had married his high school sweetheart, Kathryn, right after college and now had two children under the age of five. Kathryn was a pediatrician and Thomas's political polar opposite, but somehow it worked. Neil was a gifted pianist who, if the woman on his arm was anything to go by, was still dating women who looked exactly like Linda, the woman who'd broken his heart a few years earlier.

Introductions were quickly made and Thomas asked if Lance and Willa would join them. Willa seemed okay with the idea, so Lance said, "We'd love to."

As they walked around the fair, Lance watched his two friends with their women. Thomas and Kathryn had a naturalness to their relationship. Even while they bickered, their respect and love for each other was clear.

In comparison, it was a little sad to watch Neil with . . . *What did she say her name was? I guess it doesn't matter as long as I don't accidentally call her Linda.*

He wondered if Neil was telling himself the same thing.

The day flowed into the six of them going to a casual dinner, which led to drinks at a terrace bar overlooking the Charles River. Lance loved watching Willa with his friends. She could debate everything from politics to what survival items everyone should have on hand in case of a zombie apocalypse. After a few drinks, her opinion became more heated, but, even while she was disagreeing with someone, she still had them smiling.

When Willa excused herself to go to the ladies' room,

Thomas said, "I like her."

They'd all had a few too many drinks, evidenced by how the usually reserved Kathryn leaned toward Lance and said, "Me, too. You've been stuck on her since college. I hope you close the deal this time."

Neil drank down a gulp of his beer. "If you love her, don't let anything come between you. After you lose something like that, nothing and no one can ever compare."

Love? I don't... Lance barely had time to deny it to himself before the brunette beside Neil threw down her napkin, grabbed her purse and stood. "That's just great."

She stood there looking at Neil as if waiting for him to say something that would make her stay. He shrugged awkwardly. "I didn't mean it that way."

Hitching her purse on her shoulder, the woman raised her chin proudly and said, "The problem is, you did." She walked away without another word.

Neil finished his beer in one swig. "I could go after her, but you know what, I don't care enough to. That's what I'm saying, Lance. When it's wrong, it doesn't matter. When it's right, the thought of losing her hurts like having your testicles shoved into a blender."

"That's a disturbing image," Lance said in an attempt to lighten the mood.

"Easy, Neil," Thomas said with a nod toward the ladies' room. "Willa's coming back."

Kathryn patted Neil's back with sympathy. "Let's get him home, Thomas."

Thomas stood. "We shouldn't have done the tequila

shots. He can't handle them." He held out his hand to Neil. "Phone."

Neil stood and made a face at Thomas. "I'm fine."

Kathryn turned him around and took it out of the back pocket of his jeans. "You can sleep on our couch tonight, Neil, but we'll hold onto this."

Thomas added, "Friends don't let friends drunk text anyone. Come on, buddy."

Willa returned just in time for all of them to walk out of the bar together. After his friends left, Lance looked down at Willa and thought about what Neil had said. He understood how Neil felt more than he cared to admit.

Losing Willa a second time . . .

Right there on the street he pulled her to him and kissed her simply because he couldn't hold back a moment longer. Her mouth opened eagerly to his, and her hands were in his hair while his ran boldly over her curves. He pulled back, gasping for air. She went to kiss him again, but he jerked his head away.

Not like this.

He hailed a cab.

She searched his face for a long moment then went to open the door of the cab that had pulled up. He blocked her entrance with an arm. "Willa, we've both had too much to drink . . ."

She kept her face averted, but he could see that she was embarrassed. "Good night, Lance."

With a hand beneath her chin he turned her face until she was forced to look at him. "This isn't easy for me. In fact, knowing what I'm saying no to is damn near killing me."

Pride flashed in her eyes. "What you're saying no to? I kissed you. That's all."

His hand tightened on her chin. God, she was so fucking sexy. When she said yes. When she said no. He pulled her against him again. His swollen cock stretched the limits of his jeans. "You and I both know how little it would take for us to be screwing in the bushes, not caring who saw us." He kissed just below her ear. "I'm not ashamed of how you make me feel. I want you. But not like this. Not because we're both buzzed. I want to take my time. I want to fall asleep inside you because we came so many times we couldn't move. Then I'll wake up and start my day by tasting that sweet pussy of yours again."

Her breathing became as deep and labored as his. He whispered in her ear. "Yes, that's how I want to fuck you. Not like this. Go home, Willa. I'll pick you up tomorrow afternoon."

She sank into the cab, biting her bottom lip, looking dazed, turned on and so damn confused. He couldn't send her off alone in a cab that way. Swearing, he slid in beside her and closed his eyes, praying for strength. "I'll see you home, but I won't come in." The cab pulled out into traffic and Lance gave the driver directions to Willa's place.

The air of the cab was charged with sexual tension even though he and Willa were neither looking at each other nor touching. They rode in silence.

She folded her arms across her chest and said softly, "I've

never even had sex outside. Your impression of me is way off." Her chin rose. "And I'm not drunk."

It might have been the alcohol lowering his filter with her, but he put his arm along the back of the seat and leaned in. "Never?"

She blushed and met his eyes briefly before looking away. "I don't see the lure. All you're doing is giving a cheap show for perverts."

He lifted her long blonde curls and tucked them behind her shoulder, exposing that glorious neck of hers. "I don't know if anyone plans for it to happen." He spoke closer to her, letting his breath on her ear be its own caress. "And I've never seen the lure either. Until you. When I'm with you all I can think about is you. Talking to you. Holding on to you. Kissing you. And yes, fucking you. I don't care where we are or who sees us. I want to go slowly with you, and it's driving me mad. How do you do this to me? How do you make me forget everything else and just need you?"

Their eyes met and held. Her mouth parted slightly and that delicious tongue of hers licked her bottom lip nervously. "You make me feel the same way."

"Thank God." He kissed her shoulder. "We could blow off the tour tomorrow, but Emily's feelings might be hurt."

"We have to go."

"I'm on schedule at work. I could take Monday off. We could go somewhere. Just you and me."

Willa blinked slowly as she thought it over. "I have to work on Monday."

Lance kissed his way across her collarbone and to the

sweet curve of her neck. "Your boss won't fire you. Pack a bag. We'll leave from my parents' house."

Willa shook her head as if doing so would help her think. "I want to . . ."

He kissed her jaw and loved how her hand found and clenched on his thigh. "Say yes."

Willa ran her hand up and down his thigh. The back of her arm brushed across his cock and Lance shuddered from the pleasure of it. "Yes."

It took all he had not to come just from the sound of her voice. They pulled up to the front of her building. He walked her to the door but didn't kiss her. He knew he wouldn't leave if he did. Only after he knew she was safe inside did he return to the cab and give the driver directions to his apartment.

On the way there he leaned back in the seat and closed his eyes with a pained moan. *Why the hell are we spending tomorrow with my family?*

Chapter Eleven

HAND IN HAND, Willa and Lance followed Emily through her museum as she explained the origin of each piece. Now and then she stopped and put her hand on her back as if it were aching, but her smile was bright. Although Willa was far from bored, she was struggling to pay attention to what Emily was saying. She wanted to fast forward through the tour, through dinner, and give herself over to the pleasure she knew the next couple days promised.

She'd spent half the night asking herself if agreeing to go away with Lance had been a wise choice and the other half imagining how good it would be with him. It was about more than just sex, although she was looking forward to that. Everything was more vivid when he was at her side. Colors were brighter. Food tasted better. Willa's face hurt from smiling as much as she had these last couple days. *Simply holding his hand feels so damn good I don't want to let go.*

She glanced at Lance and her breath left her in a whoosh when their eyes met. He winked and gave her hand a gentle squeeze. *He's finding it as difficult to concentrate as I am.* He wiggled an eyebrow as if checking that her mind had wandered to the same naughty place his had. She tried to keep a straight face, but she couldn't. She let out a loud laugh.

Emily stopped the story she was sharing and turned toward them. She placed a hand on one hip as if she were about to reprimand the two of them, but she smiled instead. Her eyes danced with humor. "You did ask for this tour."

Lance and Willa exchanged an amused look then both tried to look contrite. Lance chuckled. Willa joined in. They might be in trouble, but they were in trouble together. Together. Willa looked down at their linked hands and marveled at how open Lance was about being with her. It took how good she felt to a whole new level.

With an indulgent shake of her head, Emily said, "I'll show you one more section, then I'll release you two lovebirds back into the wild."

As if he just realized he could be offending Emily, Lance said quickly, "We're not in a rush, Emily. This place is truly incredible."

Emily waved for them to follow. "Don't worry, I totally understand. I'm just not sure what we're doing here. Am I a chaperone? Because I feel like that parent at a school dance whose job it is to remind the kids not to maul each other in public."

Not liking that they might have repaid Emily's kindness by making her feel uncomfortable, Willa dropped Lance's hand. "Emily, I feel awful. You have no idea how much I admire you and what this museum represents."

Emily looked modestly pleased by the comment. "Coming from a fellow artist that means a lot."

Willa shook her head. "I'm not an artist."

"Asher told me you were," Emily countered, looking puzzled. "Weren't you an art major in college?"

"I studied art, but I'm not talented. I simply appreciate it."

Lance frowned. "That's not true. Kenzi was always talking about something you'd painted or the sculptures you created. She'd send me pictures of them. They were quite good."

Willa couldn't even remember the last time she'd picked up a sketch pad. "That was a long time ago and Kenzi would have loved anything I made."

Lance looked certain he was right. "Didn't you win a scholarship with one of your paintings?"

He remembers, Willa thought in awe. "I did, but there wasn't much competition that year."

Their eyes met and held. "It was more than that. I saw it. It had humor and emotion. I was amazed at how you'd been able to portray a real tension between two squirrels facing off over one acorn. It made me laugh and feel sorry for them at the same time."

Willa looked away, unsure of how to handle how much it meant to her that she'd mattered to him back then. Believing she mattered to him had died when Lexi told her about their kiss. Yet now it was cautiously coming back to life. She caught Emily watching her reaction and blushed. "Thank you, but they were nothing like what's here."

Emily tipped her head to one side and studied Willa before speaking. "I know exactly how you feel, Willa. I've spent most of my life trying not to get lost in the shadow of my mother's talent. I will probably never feel that I am as good as she was, but my sculptures are an extension of who I am, and I've learned to value that. Every piece in this museum is different and wonderful in its own way. Some way or another, they are also all a piece of my journey. Comparison is a death blow to creativity. Don't let it stop you from doing what you love." Her eyes misted over. "I dare you to give me something to display at my museum. If you still have that sketch, I'll take it. Or you can create something else."

"Oh, I can't imagine—"

"Is that how you handle a dare? You've got more fire in you than that." Lance's hand on her lower back felt possessive, daring.

Warming beneath the touch of his hand and his encouragement, Willa felt like she just might. She smiled cautiously at Emily. "Does it have to be three dimensional?"

"It's better if it is, but it doesn't have to be. My favorite works are emotional ones. Come on, let me show you the pieces I made with my mother," Emily said as she started walking again. The room she led them into was filled with prints of famous paintings and small sculptures of a part or all of what was in the painting. "These were some of my earliest ones. There was a purpose to them. As you know, my mother was born blind so she had no way of experiencing these works outside of having them described to her. In trying to find a solution for her, I found my passion. I'd love something that represents your own journey. You could do something about being a twin . . ."

Willa tensed and would have stepped back if Lance's hand wasn't still on her lower back. Without thinking about how it would sound, she spilled out what she was thinking. "Being a twin doesn't define me."

Emily's mouth dropped open in surprise, and she instantly looked apologetic. "I didn't mean to imply that it did, but it's part of who you are."

Wishing she'd held her reaction in, Willa backpedaled. "Sorry, it's just that—"

"You want to be your own person," Lance said near her ear.

He understands. Willa nodded gratefully. She thought about what Emily had said about comparison killing creativity and couldn't help but see how it had also shaped her relationship with her sister. *I've always compared myself to her. Is that what's killing our relationship?* Willa remembered the last few conversations she'd had with Lexi and realized she'd judged Lexi just as harshly. She pressed her lips together then said, "Yes, but it's more complicated than that." There was also the wonder of having someone who was so close to you, you could feel their pain or joy as your own. Or, at least, that's how it used to be when they were children. They'd lost that magic somewhere along the way, except in those rare instances when they were both excited about the same thing and they could finish each other's sentences. Even though Willa wanted to find herself, she missed that connection. *Complicated.*

Looking on sympathetically, Emily said, "If you represent what you're feeling right now in some concrete fashion, you'll have your masterpiece."

"I don't know if it would be a masterpiece, but I'll do it, Emily. I'd be honored to make something for your museum. You've inspired me." Willa meant it. Emily had laid down a challenge, and Willa admired Emily more, if that were even possible. She smiled at Lance, grateful he'd brought her. He'd said he liked the man he was when he was with her. Well, she liked the woman she was when she was with him. Even though she fluctuated between being deliriously happy and scared shitless, it was better than the bland existence she'd convinced herself she preferred. *I closed so much of myself off, telling myself it was the only way to survive. I didn't realize how much I'd lost along the way.*

Lance leaned down and whispered, "If you need a nude model . . ."

And just like that, Willa was smiling and laughing again. "You are so bad." She lost herself for a moment in his dark eyes.

Unrepentant, Lance shot her a lusty smile. "Or I could draw *you*."

"And that's the end of today's tour," Emily chirped in with a chuckle. "I'll be right back, then if you want we can drive over to your parents' place together."

Lance agreed while Willa fought back a mild panic. *I'm going to the Barrington home as Lance's . . . date? As his what? Girlfriend? Soon to be lover? Hi, Sophie and Dale. What's up? We thought we'd come over and see you before we run away and fuck like bunnies for a few days. In fact, could you pass the potatoes faster?* Lance's words from the night before came back and echoed through Willa. *"I want to take my time. I want to fall asleep inside you because we came so many times we couldn't move. Then I'll wake up and start my day by tasting that sweet pussy of yours again."* Willa shivered and got wet just thinking about the feel of his tongue delving into her sex.

Oh my God, I'm losing it.

"What are you thinking?" Lance asked.

Willa chewed her bottom lip. *Nothing I should say here.* Willa glanced at her watch, more to refocus herself than to actually check the time. *How long until we're alone?* "What time is dinner?"

"Early. Right after this?" Lance asked, looking like he was trying to decipher a message sent in code, then he smiled and slid his hand along the curve of her neck and pulled her face closer to his. "When you look at me like that I don't care about anything but this." His mouth came down and plundered hers. Willa arched forward against him, loving how hard and ready he was. Their tongues met and danced hungrily. She ran her hands greedily over his chest. He half lifted her and walked forward until her back was to the wall. With one hand kneading her jean-clad ass, he ground against her, moving his bulging erection back and forth against her crotch in a way that had them both moaning.

Willa pulled the back of his T-shirt out of his jeans. His rippling muscles were heaven beneath her hands. He pulled her shirt free also. Beneath her shirt, his thumb traced the outline of her bra before slipping beneath to cup her breast.

"They should still be in here," Emily said from the hallway.

Willa froze.

Lance lowered Willa back to the floor, adjusting her clothing as he did. "Shit."

"Oh," Emily said in surprise.

"Really, Lance? At Emily's museum?" Asher asked curtly.

Lance tucked Willa into his side. Willa buried her face for a moment in his shoulder as she tried to compose herself. He growled, "Don't be an ass, Asher."

Willa raised her head. She'd never heard Lance use that tone before, especially not with his brothers.

Asher's eyebrows shot up revealing his own surprise. "I'm an ass? I'm not the one giving the security cameras a show."

Emily's lips pressed together in a straight line. She looked as if she had something she wanted to say but was holding it in. "It doesn't matter."

Asher looked from Lance to Willa and back. "He knows it does."

Emily went up onto her tiptoes and gave her husband a quick kiss on the cheek. His attention shifted from Lance and Willa to his wife and the secret smile on her face. "You have a short memory, Mr. Barrington."

Asher pulled her into his arms gently, allowing for the space her rounded stomach required and kissed her briefly on the lips. "Maybe, but I know trouble when I see it."

Emily smiled up at her husband, her love for him shining in her eyes. "So do I, but I married him anyway." She caressed one side of his face.

With a grunt of concession, Asher looked back at Lance

and Willa. "Mom doesn't know you're a couple yet, does she?" The way he asked didn't sit right with Willa. He sounded as if he were suggesting there was still time to fix things—not be with her. His rejection stung. *What have I ever done to him? Does Sophie not like me? Think of me as good enough as a friend of the family, but not for one of her sons?*

Lance's arm tightened around Willa's waist. "I didn't tell her who I was bringing with me, no."

Asher frowned. "Find a reason to cancel."

His words stabbed through Willa.

Lance stepped away from Willa aggressively. Asher did the same with Emily. Youngest brother faced eldest, but time had leveled the playing field. They were the same height, had similar powerful builds, and both had a stubborn look on their face that implied the conversation was headed nowhere good. Between gritted teeth, Lance said, "What is your problem? Didn't you learn anything from when Kenzi brought Dax home?"

Asher's face tightened with remorse. "That was an accident."

Willa stepped forward to intervene. She hated that they were arguing over her. "It was." She laid a hand on Lance's arm.

Shaking his head angrily, Asher said, "Date her if you want, but do you have to announce it?"

Emily went to stand beside Asher. "Asher, I know you like Willa. Why are you doing this?"

"That's the problem. We all like her. When they break up—" Asher stopped himself then said, "*If* they break up, it won't only be Lance who will be affected."

Willa said hastily, "Lance, maybe he's right. I don't want to cause any issues."

Lance put his arm back around Willa as he continued to glare at Asher. He took a deep breath, then forced a smile. "Emily, thank you for the tour."

Emily looked back and forth between the brothers. "Don't let him leave like this, Asher."

"He's only angry because he knows I'm right," Asher said.

With an audible angry sound, Emily turned to Willa. "Block the door."

Willa hesitated, but something told her that when a very pregnant woman barks orders it's best to follow them. She went to stand in front of the door that led out of the room to the main hallway.

Emily paced before the two men, with one hand supporting her back. "This is ridiculous. Neither of you is leaving until you figure this out. Our baby will not come into the world with the two of you fighting like five-year-olds. Work it out."

"It's not good for the baby if you get upset, Emily," Asher said, looking white and worried.

"Too late for that," she answered with a wave of her hand. "Willa, sometimes you have to stand your ground, and this is one of those times."

Willa wasn't sure of that, but her admiration for Emily soared again. She was a lioness, taking two self-proclaimed kings of the jungle down a notch.

Lance glared at his brother. "You think you know what's best for the family? You don't. By your logic I should only date people no one cares about? How does that even fucking make sense?"

Willa wrapped her arms around herself protectively. This was a side of the Barringtons she'd never seen before. They didn't argue. They never raised their voices. At least, they never had in front of her.

Asher rubbed a hand over his forehead. "You're right."

The room fell suddenly absolutely silent.

Lance looked stunned. Emily nodded in encouragement.

Asher turned to Willa. "This isn't about you, Willa. My concern is—"

"I know," Willa said softly. "It's okay, Asher. I don't want anyone upset, either."

Asher nodded once.

Emily turned toward Lance. "Asher loves you. He really does. He's so proud of you. I know you feel the same about him. I never had brothers or sisters, but I'd like to think that if I did we would talk out our problems. You are so blessed to have each other. I can't sit back and say nothing while you tear into each other." She rubbed her stomach.

The tension seemed to ebb from Lance. He ran a hand through his hair. "And you shouldn't have to." When he looked at Asher, it wasn't with anger. "Going with Willa is probably a bad idea, but I want things to be different this time."

Asher's eyebrows shot up and Willa wanted to sink into the floor. She didn't want to look at the expressions on their faces, especially not Lance's. *How could I feel comfortable going to the Barrington's tonight now?* She looked around for the nearest exit—anywhere to hide her discomfort—but Lance was suddenly at her side, putting his arm around her waist. She was keeping her panic contained, but just barely. She hated that he could feel her shaking.

Asher crossed to his wife. He put his arms around her again and kissed her temple. "I can't imagine my life without you." He gave Willa a funny look then nodded at Lance. "Come to dinner, both of you. I want to hear about this city contract you won. I'm sure everyone else would like to hear about it, too. Everything else will figure itself out."

Lance looked down at Willa. "It's up to you."

"Me?" Willa let out a long, shaky breath. *Oh, no, if it's up to me the answer is hell no.*

"I want things to be different this time." Lance had said it more than once, and he seemed to mean it.

I want this time to be different too. I want to walk into a room on your arm, knowing that it's important to both of us that I'm there.

I want to believe in you again.

"I'd like to see your parents. I can thank them in person for the care package."

Lance smiled and hugged her to his side.

Willa glanced over at Asher and Emily who were watching them closely. *Are you thinking I should have come up with an excuse not to go? That we're making a mistake?*

I probably should run before I get in too deep. Before my heart is broken a second time.

Willa rested her cheek briefly on Lance's strong shoulder.
But I don't want to.
God help me, I still love him.

A SHORT TIME later Lance paused at the bottom of the steps at his parents' house. Yes, they'd only been on a couple dates, but theirs didn't feel like a new relationship. Walking in with her felt right.

He remembered the day Kenzi had brought Dax home. She'd taken the family aside and warned them all to be nice to him. Lance suddenly understood why. He didn't care what his family thought of his decision to see her, but he wanted them to accept her because he knew their feelings would be important to Willa.

Although they'd taken separate cars, Asher and Emily had arrived just after them and were walking up the driveway. Asher put a hand on his shoulder. "Come on."

As far as pep talks went, it wasn't the best, but it was more encouragement than Asher usually gave. The door of the house opened and his father smiled in greeting. "Right on time. Dinner is ready." When he noticed Willa he said, "Oh, you brought . . . Willa, right?"

Lance blanched at the question. A quick look at Willa's face revealed that his father's uncertainty had hurt her even though she quickly hid her feeling behind a bright smile. "That's me. It's wonderful to see you, Mr. Barrington."

Dale moved forward to welcome her with a kiss on the cheek, then stopped when he noticed that Lance was holding her hand. He gave her a peck but looked concerned when he straightened. "I had no idea you knew each other so well."

"It's all good, Dad," Lance said in a firm voice. If his father gave the slightest hint of sounding anything like Asher had earlier, he was removing Willa from the situation. She deserved better.

Willa tried to smooth the situation over. "We just had the most marvelous tour of Emily's museum."

Dale's smile returned. "That's fantastic. We're very proud of our newest daughter."

"Then you should probably let her in, Dad. It's hot as hell out here," Asher said, with one arm around his wife's waist.

Emily laughed. "I'm planning my next pregnancy for the winter months. This is horrid."

"Next?" Asher asked in a fake shocked voice that had everyone chuckling.

"Come in. Come in," Dale said, opening the door wide. "Asher, why don't you take Emily and Willa to the living room? Everyone else is already here."

Lance expected Asher to do just that. Despite how assertive each of the Barrington sons were in the business world, they bowed to Dale's authority. It might have been different if he used brute force to try to control them, but he never had. He lived his life with dignity and expected his children to do the same. There was no worse feeling than being the reason Dad's head shook with disappointment. He spoke softly, argued rationally, and when all else failed, he implemented his dark weapon—guilt.

None of his children wanted to be the reason their

mother had a second nervous breakdown and although he'd never outright said they could be, the implication was always there. Lance and his siblings came home when asked to and whenever their mother was around they acted like the happy family she needed them to be.

Kenzi was the only one to challenge that unspoken doctrine. She'd put her pent-up anger and her pain right out there for all to see. She'd demanded a more honest relationship with Sophie and was doing her best to cultivate one. There was a beauty in her courage that rocked the Barringtons like an earthquake. Kenzi challenged the relationships her brothers had both with their parents and with each other. Could they be themselves and still be a family?

The people we allow into our lives change us. Asher was no longer self-absorbed and distant. Emily had brought out a softer side of him Lance had never imagined existed in his brother.

Asher surprised Lance by saying, "Em, you and Willa head in. We'll be just a minute."

Had they been alone, Lance would have assured Willa that everything would be fine. He wasn't entirely sure, though, that it would be. He released her hand and nodded for her to go with Emily. She didn't look like she wanted to leave him, but she did.

Once the women were out of earshot, Lance raised an open hand in request. "Dad, before you say anything . . ."

Standing shoulder to shoulder with Lance, Asher cut in, "Lance has always had a good head on his shoulders. He wouldn't bring Willa home if he wasn't serious about her."

Lance continued, "Today is important to me. It's important to Willa. I don't want to hide that I'm with her."

"He shouldn't have to," Asher said in steely voice Lance had never heard him use with his father. "He's a grown man, and Willa is a wonderful woman."

With a sideways look, Lance said, "I can handle this, Asher."

Asher shrugged, but stayed at his side. "Just be clear about what you want, Lance."

Lance looked skyward. "That's what I'm doing."

"Tell him that you understand the risk, but what you feel for Willa makes this necessary."

"How *do* you feel about her?" his father asked in his deep, *don't feed me nonsense* tone.

"I don't know yet, Dad—"

"I would have gone with something more definitive," Asher added dryly.

"But I know I want to give whatever we have a real chance. I want to lay a strong foundation for it. She needs to know that I care about her. That's the reason I brought her today. If that upsets anyone, they'll have to get over it." Lance ended his impassioned explanation by crossing his arms over his chest. He braced himself for his father's reaction. Willa deserved to feel valued, no matter where their time together led. He refused to feel badly about bringing her home as a way to do that.

His father blinked slowly a few times as if processing the scene before him. "Asher's right, Lance. You've always made sensible choices. Willa's a sweet woman who has been a good friend to your sister. I'm proud of you for treating her as you are."

Lance nodded and relaxed. He doubted his father would approve of how he planned to spend the next couple days with Willa, but that was one topic that didn't require disclosure.

"Are we good?" Asher asked.

Dale made a pained face. "I had a question for Lance which was the reason I wanted a moment alone with him."

"About?" Lance didn't like the expression on his father's face. Something was brewing.

"Dax had an interesting reaction when he came in with Kenzi and we told him you were bringing someone with you today. He wanted to know who it was. I said I didn't know, and I could tell he wasn't pleased with the answer. Kenzi was happy, so I'm assuming she knew it was Willa. I don't understand Dax's reaction. Is anything going on between the two of you that I should know about?"

"Nothing that I know of, Dad," Lance answered honestly. *Unless his nose is out of joint that Willa chose me and not his friend, but it's hard to imagine him caring.*

Dale laid a hand on Lance's shoulder. "You know you could tell me."

"There's nothing, Dad."

Asher shrugged and said, "I haven't heard anything."

"Okay," Dale said with a sigh. "Just tread lightly around him today. He might be upset about something completely unrelated to you, Lance, but I don't want another brawl erupting with you boys. Not here. Not anywhere. I've never seen Kenzi this happy."

The three men walked farther into the house to the living room where his family had gathered before dinner. Willa was seated next to Kenzi and Emily on a couch just across from his mother. Ian, Grant, and Dax were off to one side, talking. They all turned and looked over as Lance, Asher, and their father entered. Willa smiled, and this time it was a genuine one that lit up her eyes as well. Even here, in his family, Willa fit, and it warmed Lance's heart.

He walked up behind the couch, bent to give Kenzi a kiss on the cheek, then gave Willa one as well. She blushed, but looked pleased. He crossed over to greet his mother who was smiling from ear to ear. When he leaned down to kiss her cheek, she said softly, "Good choice, son. I always hoped you would end up with her."

He murmured back, "It's just dinner, Mom."

She took both of his cheeks between her hands. "You've made me very happy."

Lance smiled and straightened. At least someone was happy to see him with Willa. He headed over to where his brothers were standing with Dax. As soon as his eyes met his future brother-in-law's, Lance knew his father's instincts were spot on. If looks could kill, Lance would have been lying in a pool of his own blood.

Asher looked back and forth from Lance to Dax and strode over to stand between them. Asher's eyes narrowed at Dax in warning. Dax looked back, unimpressed. The smile he shot at Lance was little more than a baring of teeth.

Grant was the first to speak. "I always knew you had a

sweet spot for Willa."

Ian added, "I'll miss watching you pretend not to moon over her. I'm surprised you lasted as long as you did. I know we told you to stay away from Kenzi's friends, but who knew you'd listen?"

Dax's hand clenched on his beer mug. "How a man treats women says a lot about who he is."

"Yes, it does," Lance said slowly. Did Dax know about what had happened back in Nantucket all those years ago? Willa might have told Kenzi. Kenzi might have told Dax. Sleeping with Willa back then, taking her virginity, wasn't something Lance was proud of, but he also didn't consider it any of Dax's business. "Which is why I brought her here today. We just started dating, but I don't want to hide it."

"How good of you," Dax growled.

Lance threw up a hand. "Do you have a problem with me?"

"Many," Dax said, then looked across at where the women were sitting. "But I'm trying to keep them to myself."

"Try harder," Asher said in a low, threatening voice.

Grant glanced at his father and mother. "This isn't the place to do this. Dax, if you have an issue with Lance take it up with him later."

In his smooth, politician-style voice, Ian said, "There are always two sides to every story. Dax, whatever you think you've heard about Lance, it's probably wrong. As a kid, he wouldn't even step on ants for fun. So, I'd question your source."

His hands clenching at his sides, Dax growled, "My

source has no reason to lie, and I don't have to tell Lance what he did. He knows. What he doesn't know is that being Kenzi's brother won't protect him if he fucks up again."

All three of his brothers turned their eyes on Lance as if he were suddenly on trial. Lance wasn't sure if Dax was referring to Willa, but he intended to find out. "Why don't we step outside and talk, Dax?" Lance suggested between clenched teeth.

Dax shook his head. "I'm not sure I could do that without sending my fist down your throat. I don't want to hear your side, and I don't need to say anything more, because we now have an understanding, don't we?" With that, Dax walked away and went to sit beside Kenzi.

Asher frowned at Lance. "What the fuck did you do?"

Grant weighed the possibilities, then said, "Kenzi had to have said something to Dax. Did you say something to upset her?"

Lance didn't respond. His mind was racing. He and Kenzi were on good terms. This had to be about Willa. It didn't add up. Why would Kenzi act like she wanted Lance to go out with her friend, but then tell Dax she didn't want him to?

Ian pocketed his hands and rocked back onto his heels. "You need to figure it out before it blows up in your face, Lance. Fix it. There's no winning in this situation. If we side with you, we side against Kenzi. We can't do that."

Asher flexed his hands. "I could take Dax."

Grant sighed. "No one is *taking* anyone. Something obviously upset Dax. Are you sure you don't know what he's talking about, Lance?"

Lance lifted and dropped a shoulder. "Why would I lie?" He looked over and caught Willa's eye. She had been laughing but suddenly looked concerned when she saw his expression. He forced a smile to his lips. "Willa and I were together briefly, a long time ago. Kenzi might have told him about that, but his reaction is extreme to say the least."

Looking as if he was trying to solve a puzzle, Grant added, "Unless Willa said something to him. She works in his office now, doesn't she? Is she upset with you about something?"

Lance met Willa's eyes across the room. He wanted to say no, but he wasn't sure. He remembered what she'd said about the past being too much for her to be able to deal with.

Because she was a virgin?

Because I kissed her sister?

Was it what I said to her later out of anger?

She wouldn't tell Dax any of that, would she?

And, if that's it, I will feed Dax's fist right back to him. He's no fucking saint, and we welcomed him into our family.

From Willa's expression, it was obvious she knew Lance wasn't happy. He tried to reassure her silently. It wasn't something he wanted to discuss with her right then, but they'd be alone soon enough.

Why, Willa? What is it that Dax knows that you haven't shared with me? You said you were willing to start fresh.

Dale walked over to join his sons. "Is everything all right?"

When none of them answered him, his gaze flew to where Dax and Kenzi were sitting. "He's family now or very soon will be. Whatever is going on, you need to settle it in a way that doesn't change that."

Chapter Twelve

➤➤➤⋘⋘

WILLA WAS RELIEVED when, after dinner, everyone flowed into the living room for coffee. Even though the meal itself had been perfectly executed by the Barrington's cook, Willa had barely touched any of the courses. There was tension at the table that she couldn't help feeling she was the cause of.

Lance hadn't left her side, but not in the flirtatious, attentive way that would have left her smiling. He hovered over her protectively, which only put her more on edge. *Does he regret bringing me?*

Only the women in the room seemed happy with how the evening was going. The men kept their expressions carefully neutral. Willa didn't know what had been said, but she prayed Dax hadn't said anything. The look of disgust in his eyes when Lance spoke made her nervous that he had.

Why did I ever say anything?

Who needs enemies when I can sabotage my own happiness?

Willa wasn't sure what to think when Emily pulled her off to the side. "Can I ask you a question?"

I'm not saying anything. I've already said too much. "Sure,"

Willa answered.

"Kenzi told me you were reading her aunt's journal. I wanted to ask you what you thought."

Journal? Oh, yes. "I was supposed to, but it never happened. Why?"

Emily placed her hand on her stomach. "I could be paranoid because I have baby on the brain, but I still get goosebumps every time I think about how obsessed their aunt was with Sophie's last pregnancy. She hated her so much for having a girl when she'd never had one herself. Then all those numbers. They have to mean something." She lowered her voice to a whisper. "To have a nasty woman like that fixated on your babies and then for one of them to die—" She shuddered. "What if she did something to the baby?"

"Kenzi's twin died in the hospital from premature complications." Even as Willa said it, her stomach lurched. She didn't want to think about babies, not having them, not losing them.

"Asher doesn't want to talk about it. Do you know if they were given the body?" Emily's eyes were large and round.

Whoa, that came out of nowhere. "I think Kenzi said he was buried with Dale's family." Willa said softly. The last thing she wanted to do was be caught talking about Kent during what was already an awkward evening.

Emily let out a relieved breath. "Oh, good. That puts my mind at ease. I know how taboo this subject is, but I couldn't stop thinking about it. That journal could be used in psychology courses as an example of how a sociopath thinks. She was a nasty woman. I'm glad I never met her."

"I don't know that Kenzi or her brothers ever did, either. Sophie distanced her children from her sister's family."

"She was smart to." Emily laughed nervously. "I'm sorry I even brought it up, but I didn't want to say anything in front of Lance. I don't want anyone to think I'm looking for trouble. They've all warmly accepted me, and I couldn't be happier. I'll drop this now. If the past holds any secrets, maybe they're better left alone."

Willa smiled weakly. Her eyes darted from Dax to Lance. *I couldn't agree more.*

FROM ACROSS THE room, Lance frowned as he watched Emily and Willa have a private conversation. He didn't know what they were talking about, but it was something that looked like it was making Willa uncomfortable. Lance didn't like confrontation, but he liked secrets even less.

In an amused voice, Kenzi said, "You and Willa make a cute couple."

"We're not yet a couple. Not officially."

"But you brought her here."

"I did," Lance said. He was a planner who always factored the worst-case scenario into his strategy. When it came to being with Willa, that side of him seemed to turn off. He went from one misstep to the next. "It doesn't mean what everyone seems to think it does."

Kenzi's eyes darted to his. "What *does* it mean?"

"That I like her, and I don't care who knows. That I

want to date her and see where it goes. Does it have to be more than that?"

Kenzi leaned against Lance and hugged him. "No, it doesn't. That sounds like a nice place to start."

Dax looked over at them then looked away. The way Kenzi tensed beside Lance told him she was aware that there was a problem. *Might as well address it.* "Your fiancé keeps looking at me like he'd enjoy wringing my neck. Is there something you're not telling me?"

Kenzi chewed her bottom lip. "Willa said something to Dax last week. I don't know the details because she asked him not to say anything to me. He almost didn't, but he was worried and wanted to make sure I knew to check in on her. He wouldn't tell me why she was upset, but it has something to do with you. I know he doesn't always show it the way we would, but Dax cares about us. All of us. He's also very protective, especially after I shared what happened to me. Did you and Willa have an argument?"

"No. We've actually been getting on really well." Lance's thoughts did a tailspin. He went over the past couple of days with her. Was it possible that she wasn't enjoying their time together as much as he was? It was a question he'd never had to ask himself with other women, but with Willa he wasn't sure.

Confused, Kenzi shook her head. "He might have misunderstood something she said. I haven't had the chance to talk to her about it yet, and as she had asked Dax not to tell me, I don't feel I can ask her yet. She's a private person, Lance."

But she opens up to Dax? "I don't understand Willa."

Kenzi's expression turned sympathetic. "Give yourself time. Give *her* time. When she's ready, she'll open up and let you in." She looked across to Dax. "And I'll talk to Dax."

Lance wanted to storm over and demand that Willa tell him what she'd said to Dax, but he didn't. He'd repeatedly asked Willa why she was still upset with him. They could go around and around that subject a hundred more times, and he was sure she wouldn't tell him.

But apparently she told Dax.

He looked down at Kenzi and remembered how he'd felt the day he'd heard what had happened to her in high school. She'd hidden that pain from everyone, and it had nearly destroyed her.

Willa had said her feelings ten years ago had been real. Was that the pain festering within her? Had he hurt her that badly?

She came to me that night. I didn't pursue her. Maybe I wasn't ready to jump out of bed and into a relationship, but how long do I have to fucking apologize for being twenty and stupid?

I don't need this. Let her keep her secrets and her grudges.

Things were a hell of a lot simpler without her.

His eyes were drawn to where Willa was talking to Grant and his parents. She said something that made them laugh. Emily walked over with Asher, and it looked like Willa was asked to start the story over. He could watch her forever and never get bored. The way she tipped her head to listen. The huge smile that came easily to her sweet lips. Images of how she'd look, freshly fucked, spread across his bed surged through his mind.

No other woman had ever compared to her.

He doubted any ever would.

I'm going to fucking end up like Neil. He made a frustrated growl deep in his chest. *I need to slow down before we crash and burn again.*

"I hope I didn't make the situation worse." Kenzi hugged his arm.

Lance laid his hand on his sister's. "You didn't." He noticed Dax watching them and asked, "I need to talk to Dax, though."

Kenzi looked across at Dax with love in her eyes. "I think that's a good idea, but don't sugarcoat anything. He'd rather know the truth, even if it's not pretty."

Finally, something Dax and I are in complete agreement over.

Before Lance had a chance to do anything, though, Willa came over to join him. Her cheeks were flushed from laughing with his family, and it was difficult to think about anything past how he felt when she smiled and laced her fingers through his. "I was telling your parents about the first apartment Lexi and I rented together. Do you remember it, Kenzi?"

Kenzi smiled and made a small square with both of her hands. "It was so tiny you used to joke that people had to take numbers if more than one wanted to visit."

Willa chuckled. "I had this old trunk I'd bought at a yard sale. I thought it would be the perfect post-college storage solution until we couldn't find a place for it in the apartment."

"So you tried to wedge it in the closet," Kenzi said, her eyes sparkling with amusement.

Laughing harder, Willa met Lance's eyes. "And I got my arms stuck between it and the wall."

Drawn into the fun of the memory, Lance let everything else fall away. "What did you do?"

"My cell phone was in my back pocket."

"So, she hopped up and down until it fell out," Kenzi added.

"Which was not an easy feat, but I did it," Willa said with pride. "Then I kicked off my shoes and socks—"

"And called me," Kenzi finished, laughing so hard she was gasping for air. "I think I still have that photo saved somewhere."

Waving a finger in warning, Willa warned, "What kind of friend takes a picture before they rescue you? Your sister, Lance, that's who. Bring it on, Kenzi. Payback will be fun. I have quite a collection of blackmail photos of you."

"She does," Kenzi said with a laugh. "She gets photo happy sometimes. Which was why I had to take the opportunity when it was presented." She held her side. "Oh, God, I haven't laughed that hard in a while. What brought up that story?"

Willa shrugged. "Sophie asked me if I liked where I was living. I told her that it is a lot better than some of the places we've rented. It's double the size of our last place. I don't know why I remembered the day with the trunk, but I did.

She thought it was hilarious."

Kenzi chuckled again. "She adores you. I saw Grant laughing. Tell me he didn't—"

"Offer to look over my stock portfolio and give suggestions? He can't help himself." Willa met Lance's eyes again, and her smile widened. "Grant never understood that Lexi and I are Kenzi's poor friends. I'd show him my bank account balance, but I'm afraid he'd have a heart attack."

Lance frowned. He didn't like the idea of Willa struggling financially. He almost asked her if Dax was paying her a good salary but decided against it. He considered offering her money, but thought that might not go over well, either.

Slow. Remember. Take it slow.

As she spoke, she leaned against him and the side of her breast brushed against his arm and the devil in him won. His blood started pounding, and he found it difficult to concentrate on anything other than how good she felt—how good she would taste.

I'm definitely going to hell.
Unless I'm already there.

Chapter Thirteen

>>>><<<<

AN HOUR LATER, Willa turned in the passenger seat of Lance's car and rested her head in a way that allowed her to watch him as he drove. The night had gone better than she'd hoped it could. Yes, it had started off feeling stilted, but after the meal everyone had relaxed. Her worry that Dax would say something abated, and she'd actually had fun. Lance had smiled and laughed with her.

So why do I get the feeling he's not happy with me?

When Lance had picked her up that morning he'd mentioned that he rented a house on Cape Cod for the weekend. He said it was right on the beach, which was why he'd chosen the place. That and the indoor pool. He'd followed up that statement by asking her if she'd ever gone swimming naked. Her answer that she hadn't had put a lusty smile on his face and a blush on hers.

Willa was working on not overthinking things, not worrying about every last thing that could go wrong. When she'd told Dax she was taking Monday off, she hadn't told him it was because she would be away with Lance. There was a chance she would lose the best-paying job she'd ever had for—a taste of heaven? Normally the idea of risking any employment would have made her sick to her stomach, but this was different. This was Lance. A decade of thinking about him, secretly dreaming that something like this would one day happen.

She would have felt better about her decision if Lance was holding her hand. He wasn't flirting with her. In fact, he was barely talking at all.

"Hey," she said softly.

He smiled, but it didn't reach his eyes. "Is for horses."

"That's so corny." His smile faded and she kicked herself internally for critiquing instead of saying something that would have had him laughing again. "I had a good night."

He glanced at her then back at the road. "It was different than I expected."

The way he said it was like a lead stone settling onto her chest. "In what way?"

She wished she hadn't been watching him so closely because then she might not have seen the flash of disappointment in his eyes. "I'm dropping you back at your place, Willa."

"Why?" she asked in a calm voice even though what she really wanted to do was grab the wheel, pull the car to the side of the road and demand he look at her.

"We said we'd take it slowly then planned a few days of the exact opposite."

Feeling cold, Willa wrapped her arms around herself. "I don't remember complaining."

He opened his mouth then snapped it shut as if deciding

to hold back a comment. Willa's stomach churned as she grew nervous. The longer he was quiet, the sicker she felt. His jaw tightened visibly, and he kept his eyes on the road ahead. "Did you say something to Dax about us?"

Oh, shit. "Yes." *What are the chances that answer will suffice? A girl can hope.*

"I thought we had fun this weekend."

"We did."

"Then explain to me what I'm doing that is so wrong that you complained to my sister's fiancé about it?"

Fighting back tears, Willa said, "You're not doing anything wrong."

Lance's knuckles turned white on the steering wheel. "I want to understand you, Willa. I really want to, but I'm lost."

"Dax misunderstood something I said. I was upset, and he assumed he knew why. I tried to tell him he was wrong. I thought I was clear, but maybe I wasn't. He shouldn't have said anything to you. In fact, he promised he wouldn't." Willa turned to face forward as she realized she shouldn't have said the last part. It made it sound like she was keeping something from Lance. She was, but she didn't want him to know that.

"He was worried about you. What I want to know is why."

"It was before I talked to you on Thursday night."

"And?"

"And Clay was asking me about you."

"You talked to Clay about us?"

"No. Yes." Willa covered her face with one hand. *I can't do this. I'm not ready to do this.* "You're right. You should just drop me off at home."

Lance pulled onto a side street and parked. In a much softer tone, he took one of her hands in his. "Help me understand."

Is this where I tell him about the pregnancy? About how I debated telling him for weeks. Do I lead with the miscarriage or how I hated myself because even though I had decided to keep the baby a part of me was relieved when I lost it?

Do I tell him that for a long time I blamed him for every mistake I made, every wrong man I slept with?

How because of him I almost turned my back on my sister?

That even now, even when I know none of that was his fault, a part of me is still angry with him—with myself. And so afraid I'll lose myself again? "I can't do this, Lance. Please, just drive me home."

His face contorted with pain. "And if I do, what then? We go back to pretending we feel nothing for each other? Is that what you want?"

"I don't know." She stared out the window of the car only because looking at Lance hurt too much. She gathered her thoughts the best she could. Every moment with Lance felt right. They fit together in a way she'd never imagined they could. Not even back when she'd fantasized about being with him. Whether it was walking hand in hand through an art fair, or laughing over drinks with his friends, she wanted more of him in her life. With him, she didn't compare herself to Lexi. With him, she felt beautiful and life felt full of possibility. *I like who I am when I'm with him.* She turned back to meet his eyes. "I do know. I don't want to go back to how things were."

Lance expelled a breath, but he didn't make a move to touch her. "Structures are only as strong as their foundation. If we can't be honest with each other, what can we build on that?"

Willa let his words sink in and clasped her hands on her lap. *I have to tell him. It's time.*

Oh, God, don't let me lose him over this.

Please, give me the words that will help him understand. "I fell apart after we slept together. Lexi and I had a huge argument, unlike any we've ever had." Willa's eyes filled with tears. "She's the only family I have, really, and I thought I'd lost her. I was devastated. I was so sad, so angry . . . I made mistakes. I did so many things I wish I could go back and undo." Willa hesitated. He'd asked for honesty, but wasn't that what everyone said just before they were told something that changed everything? *Here goes . . .* "I hated you. I blamed you because I couldn't stay angry with Lexi and not lose her, so I hated you instead." One tear spilled down her cheek then another. "I hated myself just as much, though. When I look back at that time, I start to unravel. Talking to you Thursday morning had me thinking about the past, and then I was falling apart on the inside again. That's what happened in front of Clay and Dax. I let the memories get to me." Her shoulders started to shake as she prepared to tell him the part she dreaded the most. "I'm sorry. I'm so sorry."

Lance released his seatbelt, undid hers and pulled her

into his arms. "It's okay, Willa. You don't have to do this."

Tucked against his strong chest, hearing his murmured words of comfort, Willa finally let her pain out. She cried for the young woman who had given him her heart and had it broken. She cried because this was exactly who she didn't want to be with Lance. She knew his family history and how one woman's sorrow had shaped his home life. She wanted to be happy for him. She didn't want to lay more guilt at his door. That wasn't the foundation she wanted their relationship built on. She hated that she couldn't contain her sorrow. It poured out of her until she was shaken and drained.

And I haven't even told him about the baby. She straightened, dug in her purse for a tissue, and took a deep breath. If it changed how he felt about her, at least it was out there. "Lance, I need to tell you one more thing—"

Lance laid a hand on one side of her face and covered her mouth lightly with a thumb. "No, you don't. I understand now. You don't have to go back to that time. Ever again. It has no power in the here and now. The last forty-eight hours have been incredible. With you. I want more of you. Say you want the same and let's move forward. Together."

The tenderness in his eyes hadn't been there before, certainly not after they'd left his parents' house. If she wasn't completely positive that it couldn't be true, she would have said he looked like a man who was falling in love. *Wishful thinking. I need to finish the story. Just say it.*

"Say it," Lance prompted. "Say you want me as much as I want you. I don't mean just in bed. This weekend has been incredible. My friends love you. My family loves you. I—" He stopped, then said, "I feel good when I'm with you. I don't know where this is going, but I don't want to give up on it."

She could have circled back to sharing her pain, but that would have completely changed where the conversation was going. She wanted the promise of happiness he was offering. She took his hand in hers and kissed his palm before lowering it to her lap. "Me neither."

The kiss she was rewarded with was heartbreakingly tender. When he raised his head, he asked, "Where do we go from here, Willa?"

She closed her eyes briefly. *I'm a good person. Maybe not a perfect one, but surely I deserve happiness. Lexi always tells me I'm the one who holds myself back. What would happen if I just trusted that it will work out and jumped?* She opened her eyes and raised them to his. "Cape Cod?"

THOSE TWO WORDS echoed through Lance. Outwardly he was holding it together, but inside he was a wreck. Her tears had stormed through his heart like Godzilla let loose on a seaside town. There was no defense against how she made him feel. While she cried against his chest, he'd wanted to make all sorts of declarations he had no business uttering yet. He'd wanted to promise her he'd spend his life making sure she never had a reason to cry like that again. For just a few moments, forever felt possible.

Then sanity returned. They'd only actually been together a few days. He was a man who kept lunchmeat longer than most of his relationships lasted. They'd never been a priority to him.

What if being with her didn't change that side of him?

Was she the one he was meant to be with?

Or did he just want to fuck her so badly that all sense had left him?

I should know how I feel before we go further.

I should be sure.

But she said yes.

He'd promised her next to nothing, and she'd still said yes. He fought the urge to roll down the window of the car and yell that she was finally his.

It was a primal desire that brought a small smile to his lips. He was a rational man. A careful man. That's not how he felt when he was with Willa. They had a bond as old as time itself. His mind told him to take his time, not to be reckless.

His body screamed that she was his woman. *His*. It defied logical explanation, which was the source of the war within him.

He didn't consider himself a selfish man, but even as he told himself taking Willa to Cape Cod was about putting his needs above hers—he couldn't convince himself to drive her home.

Not when he could spend the night kissing her sweet lips, exploring that amazing body of hers. He wanted to be the reason she lost control—his name the one she cried out as she climaxed.

He could have her in bed with him in less than an hour.

All he had to do was stop asking himself if she needed more time. She'd said she didn't.

He thought back to what his sister had said about Dax being protective of her. He understood him better now. As much as Lance wanted to have Willa, he also wanted to protect her—from anything that would hurt her, even if that was himself.

When he didn't immediately answer Willa, her eyes fell from his, and she moved fully back into her seat. He turned forward and belted himself back in. She did the same with a click. With his hands once again on the steering wheel, Lance pulled the car back out into traffic.

He headed in the direction of the highway. He knew he should say something, but he was waiting for his thoughts to settle. He glanced at her face and then his in the rearview mirror. He doubted there were two more miserable-looking, turned-on people in Boston.

It shouldn't be like this. No matter where we take this, her happiness is what matters most.

He thought about how she'd looked as she'd told a funny story to his family. He sorted through his memories until he came across one he knew would make her laugh. "Asher used to wear Superman underwear. He thought it gave him special powers. Ian teased him mercilessly about it. I don't know when Asher finally stopped wearing them, but he's older in every retelling. If you ever want to see him squirm, ask him about them in front of my mother. She thinks it was adorable. I'm waiting for just the right time to tell that story to Emily. I was thinking when I give her a pack of super-hero diapers at the baby shower."

A smile returned to Willa's face. "He'll kill you."

Lance shrugged. "Emily would never let him. Besides, he's getting old. I can outrun him." He held out his hand to Willa. She placed hers in his without hesitation.

"Emily's definitely a good match for him. I didn't know what to do when she told me to block the door at the museum. I'm not like that. She knows how to get what she wants."

Caressing the delicate bones in her wrist, Lance said, "Normally, I would say I do, too, but you've always been able to turn me inside out." He took her hand and laid it across his bulging erection. "And turn me on."

She gasped softly and bit her bottom lip, but her hand curled around him. "What are you saying?"

He ran a hand up her thigh and gripped it possessively. "I hope we make it to the Cape."

Chapter Fourteen

>>>><<<<

THE PROPERTY MANAGER who met them with the key to the beach house gave up trying to hold Willa and Lance's attention and hung the key on a hook by the door. A man in a suit carried their luggage in and asked them if they needed anything else. Lance tipped him but declined his services.

As soon as the door closed, Lance locked it. The smile he gave Willa was deliciously decadent and perfectly represented how she felt. He loosened his tie and tossed it behind him. Then he made quick work of unbuttoning and removing his shirt. The wide smooth expanse of his muscular chest took her breath away. There was no missing the bulging evidence of how much he wanted her, or that they'd reached a place of no return. It was both exciting and a little overwhelming.

She thought he was going to move on to the belt of his trousers, but he wiggled an eyebrow suggestively at her. Mesmerized by him and unsure if he was asking her to strip for him or do something provocative, she stood frozen. A lifetime of inhibitions stood between her and the way she imagined she would be with him.

He dipped a hand into one of his pockets and pulled out a strip of condoms. They opened in an accordion-like fashion from his hand to the floor and his mouth curled with boyish charm. There were at least twenty on the strip. "Too much?" he joked.

Willa chuckled, then she let out a full laugh. Just like that her nervousness fell away. This was Lance. The real him, not the perfect version he presented to his family. He was still the best of what she'd always known about him, but funny, too. And sweet. Playful in a way she'd never imagined. As much as they were becoming lovers, they were also becoming friends. She pretended to count on her fingers. "For one night? Not nearly enough." With a smile that could not be suppressed, she pulled her shirt over her head and threw it at him. It landed in front of him like a dare.

He slung the strip of condoms over his shoulder and made short work of his shoes and socks.

She did the same then undid her bra. The heat she saw flare in his eyes at the sight of her bare breasts increased her confidence. He took what looked like an involuntary step forward when she unfastened the top of her pants.

She considered taking off each of the remaining articles of clothing one at a time, but instead stepped out of both. She stood naked before him, barely breathing, feeling the caress of his gaze as surely as if he'd been touching her.

"You're even more beautiful than I remember," he said huskily as he closed the distance between them. His mouth closed on hers, and Willa was lost to the desire that rocketed through him. *This. This has been what I've been waiting for.*

To come alive beneath a man's touch. To feel the kind of passion people write songs about.

She vaguely remembered ripping at his belt to release him. She wasn't sure if she finished the job or he did. His tongue was bold and demanding, plunging into her mouth and pulling her into an intimate dance she instinctively knew every step to.

When his freed cock nudged against her stomach, it should have been too much, too fast, but it was the opposite. Her hands couldn't get enough of him. She dug her fingers into the muscles of his back, found his hard, rounded ass, and reveled at the promise of power.

He kissed his way down her neck to her breasts. He teased with an expertise that sent her over the edge. Although she could tell he was trying to take his time, she didn't want him to. She was out of her mind and wanted him just as much as he wanted her. *Wild.* She sunk to her knees and took him deep into her mouth. He groaned and dug his hands into the hair on the back of her head.

He was big, so big, and the taste of him was like coming home. She sucked him deeper, harder, until he roughly pulled her back to her feet.

He opened a foil package and slid a condom on his large shaft before turning his attention back to her. His mouth found hers again, and she wrapped her arms around his neck. He picked her up and slid her down his chest until her sex was just about at the tip of his cock. He raised and lowered her, sliding himself deeper within her folds until he was caressing her clit with his length.

Willa wrapped her legs around his waist and opened herself wider to him. He shifted and plunged inside her with one powerful thrust that had her crying out in an animalistic way. He stepped forward until her back was against the wall of the foyer. This was no longer a gentle taking, it was a wild mating. He thrust up and into her powerfully while fucking her mouth with his tongue. She clung to him, greedy to take him deeper into her, to be filled by him.

He adjusted her so she arched backward over his arm, and he suckled at her breast while continuing to pound into her. A fire, unlike any she'd ever felt, seared through her. She dug her nails into his shoulders and came with a cry. He didn't break stride, but her pleasure drove him even more out of control. His hands bit into her and the power of his thrust was so good it almost hurt.

She writhed against him, kissing every part of him she could reach with her mouth. The taste of him, the feel of him, was so much better than she'd imagined. She felt herself rising toward her second climax and this time told him.

His pace increased, and she was back against the wall to be fucked like both of their lives depended on it, and in that moment it felt as if hers did.

He came with a groan but kept moving deeply as she gave herself over to her second orgasm. Still joined, sweaty and shaking, they tried to catch their breath. He kissed her shoulder. "I'm sorry. I meant to—"

"Shut up," she growled, pulling his head up by his hair. "It was perfect."

As she realized how blunt she'd been, she blushed, but he

caught her chin with one hand before she could turn away in embarrassment. "Yes, it was." The kiss he gave her was every bit as passionate as what they'd just done.

She felt him begin to harden inside her again.

He groaned and pulled out. "I'll be right back." He whipped the condom off, and stepped away for a moment. When he returned she had barely moved.

Still under his spell, she dropped to her knees again and took him back into her mouth. Never in her life had any man tasted as good or had going down on him felt so right. She took him as deep as possible, loving how hard he became.

He sank to his knees and pushed her onto her back. The foyer carpet tickled her, but it was quickly forgotten as his tongue found and circled her clit. He took his time, exploring her, learning what drove her wild, then took her to a place she didn't think was possible. By the time he donned another condom, she was a limp vessel awaiting his taking. He positioned himself above her and moved in and out of her slowly. They kissed on and on, in no rush this time, as he stroked her with his hands and his tongue.

When he finally came, she was in a beautiful post-orgasm glow. He rolled her over so she was on top of him and ran his hands over her lovingly. "Shit, Willa."

She would have said something, but she was beyond speech. She cuddled next to him, closed her eyes, and simply enjoyed the feel of his arms around her and his shaft within her.

LANCE WAS SHAKEN to the core. Until that moment, he thought he'd known all varieties that sex came in. It could be impatient, skillful, tender, or comfortable. He'd always made sure his partner was satisfied. Until Willa, sex had always been—civil.

He felt like a man who'd thought ice cream only came in one bland flavor then discovered what he'd thought was delicious would never again be enough.

And we haven't even made it out of the foyer. He chuckled and groaned at the same time.

Willa stirred against him. As if she could read his mind, she said, "So far I love the house."

He nuzzled her neck. "I hear there are other rooms. Even an indoor pool."

She moved sensuously against him. Every place their bodies touched was a warm reminder of the pleasure that had just rocketed through him. There was an easiness to being with her he'd never felt with another woman. He attributed it to the length of time he'd known her, but he knew it was more than that. There was a depth to sex with Willa, an emotional component that was almost terrifying. No matter what he might try to tell himself, he knew things would never be the same between them. There was no going back to pretending they didn't have feelings for each other. No way to tell himself he'd be better off without her. He ran a hand slowly up and down her bare back. His stomach rumbled. "Why did I tell the staff we didn't need them?"

She tipped her head back and nodded at their entwined legs. "It may have had something to do with this."

He rolled her beneath him, resting on his elbows above her. "That might have been it." He kissed her lips gently. "You are amazing, Willa."

She smiled up at him, surprisingly shy despite what they'd just shared. "You, too."

He knew he was grinning down at her like a dope. "I feel like I should get you off the floor."

She shifted beneath him like a cat stretching out in the sun. "Standing is overrated."

They kissed leisurely for a few long moments, then Lance eased off her. He went to the bathroom and cleaned himself off then wet a washcloth with warm water and brought it back to her. She was sitting up already so he offered her a hand. When she was standing before him he ran the warm washcloth intimately over her. She accepted his attention timidly for a moment, then relaxed and enjoyed being pampered.

She was a complicated woman, a mix of sweet and spicy. Which he was discovering as his favorite flavor. He took a step away, tossed the washcloth through the door of the bathroom and returned to her side.

For a moment, things felt awkward, but then he said, "I have an idea. Let's order pizza and go swimming while we wait for it to arrive."

"That sounds perfect." She tipped her head to the side. "Pizza, huh?"

He looked around for his phone. "I'm hungry. It's easy, and who doesn't love pizza?"

She went up on her tiptoes and kissed him. "I like this

side of you."

He smiled against her lips and grabbed her bare ass playfully. "I'm equally impressed with all of your sides, but I'll need to explore them more before I can say which is my favorite."

She slapped his hand, but she was laughing. "Order the food. I'm starving."

"Will we still have to tip him if he sees us naked?" He wasn't serious, but he loved hearing her laugh almost as much as he loved hearing her cry out in orgasm. He doubted he'd ever tire of hearing either.

With laughter shining in her eyes, she said, "You try it first, tough guy, and if you don't get arrested I'll go next."

He searched his phone for a local place, called in a quick order for a vegetarian pizza, which he knew was her favorite, then tossed his phone back on his pants. "I have a better idea. Last one to the pool answers the door." He took off in a run but came to sliding halt when he heard her call after him.

"You're not even going the right way." She sped off down a long hallway and he followed after her. He didn't even try to win. The view of her gorgeous naked ass and the triumphant smile she shot over her bare shoulder made it worth losing.

So worth losing.

Chapter Fifteen

>>><<<

EARLY THE NEXT day, Willa woke to the bright morning sun streaming into the beach house master suite's large windows. It took a moment for her to realize where she was and that the arm flung across her waist belonged to a man she'd loved, then hated, and now didn't know what she felt.

She slid out from beneath his arm, pulled on shorts and a T-shirt, and located her phone. She closed the curtains, darkening the room for Lance, and stepped out of the bedroom in search of tea. A few moments later she was seated outside on the porch with her feet pulled up in front of her. The peaceful location soothed her and added to the relaxed state great sex had already provided.

She wondered briefly if she should call Dax and apologize for taking a day off during her second week of work. It wasn't something she was proud of. It was completely irresponsible and the opposite of how she'd lived her life.

She was the one who held back, worried, and planned every step carefully.

Except for one other time, which had also involved the man asleep inside. *What would Lexi say if she knew where I was?* She'd sent her sister a vague text about going out of town overnight, but she hadn't told her with whom or where.

Because I don't trust her not to ruin this for me? We're not eighteen anymore; we have to be beyond that by now. And if we're not, we need to find a way back to how we were before. What did she say? It used to be us against the world? I don't need a partner in battle anymore, I need a sister.

Crying the day before had been cleansing. *I've kept my anger locked in a little box inside for so long because I've been too afraid to face it, but we're not children any more. With age comes the realization that talks don't have to become fights. There doesn't have to be a winner or loser. All I want is to be close with Lexi again. I should be able to call her this morning and share this part of my life with her.*

I don't know how to do that, but I have a feeling it starts with letting go of the past.

Lexi had said she'd felt badly about messing things up between Lance and her. She'd said, "I guess I thought that if my pretending to be you didn't work, then maybe you pretending to be me would." There was no denying that the flash mob scenario had somehow jump-started a second chance with Lance.

I wouldn't be here with Lance if Lexi hadn't given me a push toward him.

Willa sent an impulsive text to Lexi. **Can we do dinner this week? I miss you.**

A text message came back a moment later. **Miss you, too. When do you get back?**

Tonight.

I'll cook. Lexi's version of an olive branch. Of course, since she was an awful cook, it was also amusing.

Normally Willa would have suggested that they order something delivered, but she wanted a fresh start with her sister as well. **That sounds wonderful.** She almost placed the phone down, but instead texted, **I'm at the Cape with Lance.**

How is it going?

Amazing.

We'll talk when you get home. Stop texting and go jump the man.

Willa laughed. Classic Lexi. Feeling suddenly carefree, Willa wrote, **I would if I could still walk.**

"So this is where you went," Lance said from behind her. He bent, pushed her hair to one side and gave the back of her neck a kiss.

Willa glanced back at him. He had a pair of shorts on, but his chest was bare and his hair was delightfully still mussed from bed. "I woke up early but thought you'd want to sleep in." She placed her phone face down on the arm of the Adirondack chair.

He pulled up a chair beside hers and sank into it. "I'm an early riser, but I would have stayed in bed if you were still there." He said it as a simple fact that also just happened to be sexy and sweet at the same time. "We technically have this place until tomorrow morning, but I thought it would be easier if we went back tonight. What would you like to do today?"

Her first response was a suggestive smile which brought a twinkle to his eyes. "Oh, you mean outside of the house?"

She loved his easy chuckle. Then his expression turned

serious. "What's your idea of a perfect day at the Cape?"

It felt like the most natural thing in the world when he laced his hand with hers. "I'd like to see the area, but I've always loved quiet places like this. Lexi has our parents' adventurous gene. I'm also happy with a hammock and a good book."

"What do you like to read?"

A week ago she would have tried to think of an impressive title. She no longer felt the need to. The most amazing part of being with Lance was that he seemed to like her just the way she was. "Everything from romances to autobiographies. I'm a bit of a history junkie. If I see something in a movie or hear about it in a book I love to go back and research it."

He looked at her warmly. "E-book or paperback?"

"E-book unless I read it more than once. Then I want it in paperback so I can own it. I have a small library of signed books from my favorite authors. I started collecting them when I was in college. Right now they're boxed in a corner of my room, but one day I'd like to have a spare room I could make into a reading room with a library." Willa stopped when she felt like she'd started rambling.

"What would your dream library look like?"

She'd dreamed of one since she was a child, so this was easy to answer. She described the dark wood, the ladder on wheels, even the comfortable furniture and the fireplace she'd cuddle up in front of. It wasn't the first time she'd shared her fantasy library, but when her eyes met Lance's she felt strange about sharing it with him. He was watching her intently. Suddenly self-conscious she shrugged. "Sorry to go on and on."

"I'd love to design that library for you," he said abruptly.

Unsure of how to respond, Willa made light of his comment. "If I ever get a place big enough to have a library, I'll call you."

His hand tightened on hers. "I could buy you a house."

Willa pressed her lips together and held in her first answer. He thought he was being generous. He wouldn't understand how that kind of comment could put an ugly spin on their time together. She and Lexi had been friends with Kenzi for well over a decade and had never taken a dime from her. *I thought he knew me better than that.*

He stood, then used their linked hands to pull her to stand before him. "Say it, Willa."

She raised her eyes to his. "What?"

"I've sat back for years while you silently shot daggers at me with your eyes, and I always told myself it was better left alone. We're beyond that. If you're upset about something, say it."

If you're sure . . . "I'm offended. Just because I don't have much money doesn't mean I'm looking for a handout. I have a perfectly good life. Everyone dreams of having something special, but offering me a house made it sound like you thought I was your . . . it made me feel . . ."

He pulled her to his chest and hugged her. "I'm sorry."

Willa tipped her head back. She'd expected him to defend himself or to try to convince her that she was being too sensitive. Her irritation and self-consciousness fell away. Was it that simple? With Lance it felt as if it could be. "Apology accepted. I just didn't want you to think—"

"I don't." He took her face between his hands and kissed her tenderly. "What do you say to venturing out to find breakfast somewhere? We could walk around until it gets hot, come back and lounge in a hammock in the shade. I'm halfway through a mystery book."

She looked around. "Are there hammocks here? I didn't see any."

His smile was confident without being cocky. "There will be a large one by the time we get back."

And that's the difference between you and me, Lance. You expect everything to work out the way you want it to because that's the way it always has for you.

That's not my experience.

Life can quickly get ugly, and there isn't a damn thing you can do about it.

"But first we should shower," Lance said, then swung her up and over his shoulder. "You're coming with me, woman."

Hanging upside down, Willa pushed her panic attack aside and laughed. "Seriously? Like a sack of potatoes?"

He gave her a playful swat on the rump and said, "More like a bounty I'm claiming. Let a man have his fantasy."

Completely amused and more than a little turned on, Willa jokingly flailed against his back. "Oh, you big brute, put me down."

"Never," he growled as he carried her back into the house and started toward the bedroom with her. "You're mine."

Yes. Even though she knew he wasn't serious, Willa's stomach did a crazy flip. *I am. I always have been.*

He stopped just long enough to grab the strip of condoms from beside the bed. Once in the master bath, he lowered her to her feet and began to strip her. All jokes had fallen to the wayside along with coherent thought. It was only them and their need for each other. She helped him out of his shorts, lovingly encircling his huge, hard shaft with her hand. They stepped into the shower together but completely neglected to turn on the water. Just like everything else, it simply wasn't as important as how much they enjoyed each other.

He slammed her back against the glass wall of the shower, held her hands on either side of her head, and kissed her mouth, her neck, her breasts until she thought she'd come from that alone.

A little voice in her head warned that she needed to be careful, but she ignored it. The only fear she had at that moment was that he might stop kissing her. She was pretty sure she'd die if he did.

HOURS LATER, IN bathing suits, Lance and Willa were side by side in the large hammock he'd had installed beneath the shade of a few trees in the area of the yard that overlooked the beach below. It was close enough to provide a breeze off the water, but private enough that it felt as if they were alone on their own island.

During their drive earlier, Willa had noticed his aunt's journal sticking out the side pocket of his computer bag.

She'd asked if he still wanted her to read it and he'd said, "Yes." Although he'd gone through it, he was curious what she'd think of it. He couldn't imagine wanting to share anything so private with a woman he was sleeping with, but Willa was also a friend.

She was on a very short list of people he trusted completely.

He watched her expression turn from sympathy to disgust as she flipped through the pages. She paused just before the torn out pages and said, "What a horrible, horrible woman."

Lance couldn't agree more. "I'm glad my mother moved away from her. I've gone to quite a few family events on her side of the family and thankfully her vileness doesn't appear to be hereditary."

Willa nodded. "I met several of your cousins at the auction the night Asher proposed to Emily. They seemed like very nice people."

"Did you meet Alessandro and Victor? They're not technically related to me, but you'd never know it. When I first met them, I thought they were loud and a little too inquisitive for my taste, but they've grown on me."

Willa turned back to an earlier portion of the journal. "I think your aunt slept with Victor then married his brother."

Lance frowned. "I don't remember it saying that in there."

Flipping to another section of the journal, Willa nodded slowly as she reread. "She really disliked Victor. No woman hates a man like that unless she once loved him."

Lance tensed. He opened his mouth to ask, then shut it with a snap. Willa had said she'd once loved him. He didn't want to imagine her ever feeling that way toward him.

As if she'd heard his thoughts, Willa's eyes flew up to his. "I never hated you. I wanted to. I told myself I did, but I didn't." She ran a hand over the open pages of the journal. "Not like this. Your aunt was sick."

"I'm—"

"What do you think all the numbers mean?" Willa cut off his apology with her question.

He took hold of one side of the book so they were both holding it above them. "Some are phone numbers. The country code is for Aruba."

"Which is where your parents were when Kenzi and Kent were born?"

"Yes."

Willa shuddered against him. "The torn-out pages really bother me. She filled the rest of the book with hateful, awful thoughts. Doesn't it make you wonder what she could have written that she considered bad enough to tear out?"

"Enough that I called a couple of the phone numbers. They were either disconnected or belonged to people who'd never heard of my aunt. I felt like an idiot afterward. I don't know what I expected to uncover. I'd ask my parents about it, but you know how well that would go."

"Can I see the journal again?" Willa flipped to the part of the journal where the pages were torn out. She read the section after it. "Isn't it strange that she's obsessed with your mother and the twins she was carrying right up until the missing pages. Then she doesn't mention either again. In fact, it's almost a year before she writes anything in the journal again. It's creepy." She looked back up at Lance.

Lance took the journal and weighed it in his hand. "Do you remember the woman who came to my office and pretended to be my secretary?"

"Yes."

"She said she was disappointed in my family's lack of curiosity."

"That's an odd thing to say."

"She implied there were scandalous secrets in this book. I read it. I can't say I learned much more than that my aunt was troubled."

"That's a kind way of saying it."

"Part of me wants to go to Aruba and see if any of these other numbers mean anything. Do you think that's crazy?"

"I don't think it's crazy at all."

"You know how much it would upset my family if they found out."

"Maybe it's time to stop worrying about what they need and do something for yourself."

Lance inhaled deeply. Those same words, said by anyone else, might have sounded harsh, but they were a gentle prod from Willa. And a welcome one. "You're right. I don't like secrets. I prefer to deal with facts. You can't make a decision based on half the information."

Willa laid her head back on Lance's shoulder. "So, you'd want to know something, even if it was unpleasant and had happened a long time ago?"

He kissed her forehead and cursed himself for bringing a somber expression to her eyes. Theirs was supposed to be a passionate weekend away. He closed his eyes and hugged her to him. "It's too beautiful of a day to discuss this."

She sighed and relaxed against him. Having her tucked against him felt good. So damn good it was easy to forget everything beyond the feel of her skin against his, the soft tickle of her breath across his chest. He'd never let women sleep over at his place, but he didn't look forward to leaving Willa at her apartment when they returned to Boston. Nothing had prepared him for how good simply being with her would be.

Holy shit, she was fucking phenomenal. But that in itself was unsettling. Being with her felt like he'd just discovered his newest sports car had no brakes.

The ride was a rush, but could it end in anything but a crash?

It can if I do things differently this time.

Better.

I need to stop letting my dick make all the decisions. I wanted to take it slowly with her this time.

That plan failed.

But things are still good.

He caressed her arm absently. His thoughts wandered from the heated images of how they'd enjoyed the shower that morning to how much he'd enjoyed walking around Provincetown with her. *Maybe this is where we need to be for a while. Simply enjoying each other. We'll figure everything else out when we come down from this high.*

There's a solid plan B.

"Lance?"

"Hmm?" he answered lazily, simply enjoying the way she said his name.

"Today was wonderful."

He turned onto his side so he was face to face with her. She looked happy and well loved. He soaked in that image of her, thinking he'd never seen her more beautiful. "I agree. I hate to go back."

Her expression turned serious, and she tucked an arm beneath her head. "There's something I need to tell you before we go."

He gently tucked a loose curl behind her ear. "I'm listening."

She closed her eyes briefly as if gathering her strength, opened them again, and said, "I've held it in for so long, but I finally feel like I can say it. You've given me the strength to. There was a reason I took what happened between us so hard. It's why I stayed angry long past when I should have been over it. I was—" She swallowed visibly. "I was—"

He was about to reassure her that she could tell him anything when his phone rang. He ignored it, but it kept ringing. He swore and sent the call to voicemail before dropping the phone on the grass below the hammock. When he looked back at Willa, the hopeful expression on her face reminded him of the morning after they'd had sex all those years ago. *Shit.* He knew that expression.

He thought he would have more time, but there it was.

Love.

Everything had gone to shit when she'd said, *"I love you,"* the first time.

If she says it now, she'll expect me to say it back. And I can't. Not yet. Not if I'm honest.

I have to stop her.

Those three words were a death blow to early relationships. He'd seen it before with women who'd fallen for him. Even with Willa herself. There was no nice way to say, "I wish I felt the same."

There was also no coming back from being honest in that moment.

I won't lie to her.

It wasn't that he didn't care about Willa. He did. *But love. Holy shit. Love?*

He swung out of the hammock and only saved himself from falling flat on his face at the last minute. He picked up his phone and made a show of checking who the message was from. "I'm sorry, Willa, but this is important."

"Okay," she said, sitting up, surprised and a little disappointed.

He played the message back. It was a courtesy call from his dentist office reminding him it was time to schedule a cleaning. He pretended to call the person back and nodded as if listening to someone speaking. "Of course. I can be back in Boston in an hour. No, you were right to call me." He hung up and lied to Willa for the first time. He wasn't proud of himself for doing it, but he'd been in this place with her before and messed it up. He'd told himself he wouldn't hurt her this time, but he knew he would if he was honest with her. He wasn't ready for more yet. "Emergency at the office. We should head back now."

She gathered her things and stood. "I hope it's nothing serious."

"Nothing I can't handle." *I hope.*

"So we're leaving now?"

"Looks that way. Sorry to end our trip so abruptly."

"Don't even think about it. Things like this happen. Is there anything I can do to help?" She was so sincere, he felt awful.

They walked together to the house. "No, this is my problem."

I brought us here—again

Because ten years later, I'm still a dick.

Chapter Sixteen

WILLA CARRIED HER overnight bag up the steps of her apartment building as Lance drove off. The most passionate night of her life had just ended on an oddly formal note she couldn't understand. Lance had opened her door, retrieved her bag from his trunk, and given her a quick peck on the cheek before speeding away.

A quick peck.

He was either distracted by a serious situation at his office, or . . . she hated thinking about what else it could be. There were too many depressing options. He might be running off to another woman. He didn't have the reputation of being a love-'em-and-leave-'em guy, but the way he'd dropped her off definitely felt like a drop and ditch.

I'm being paranoid. He'll handle whatever is going on at his office then call me. We'll laugh about this.

At her apartment door, Willa dug through her purse for her keys. Dressed in jeans, a T-shirt, and an apron, Lexi opened the door while Willa was still searching. Lexi's bright smile reminded Willa of how she'd felt before the awkward hour-long car ride home, during which Lance had kept the conversation as superficial as if they were strangers chatting while waiting on a train.

"I ordered sushi, but you're earlier than I thought you'd be."

Willa placed her bag just inside the door and her keys in the bowl on the table. "So, why the apron?"

Leading the way into the living room, Lexi tossed her long hair over one shoulder. "It's psychological. When you see me in this, doesn't it make you feel like I cooked?"

The haughty tone Lexi used sent a gurgle of laughter through Willa. "It makes me question your sanity."

"I bet I could do a cooking show. I look good in an apron." Lexi struck a pose and Willa's mood lightened. If anyone else had said it, they might have come across as full of themselves, but Lexi didn't. She wasn't bragging, she was embracing a possibility and approaching it with the overabundance of confidence she'd been born with. Her wink was her way of reminding Willa to not take what she was saying or herself too seriously. Really, it was difficult to do anything but smile when Lexi turned on the charm.

"You do, Lexi. A cooking show, really? That's new. Does that mean you're no longer working at Poly-Shyn?" Willa quickly washed her hands in the kitchen sink, dried them, and headed over to the table.

Lexi poured them both a glass of wine and sat down. "I'm still there, but you know me, I like to have a backup plan."

Willa sat down and kicked off her shoes beneath the table. She wasn't a big drinker, but she needed one that night.

"I hope I still have a job in Dax's office." She took a long sip.

"Wait, you're working for Dax now? What happened to taking the job with Clay?"

Willa downed the rest of her glass and reached for the bottle to refill it. "It's a long story."

The doorbell rang. Lexi paid the delivery man and began unpacking the food onto the table. "Put something in your stomach if you're going to drink so fast. Then you can tell me everything."

Willa nodded and bit into a California roll. She chewed and swallowed before speaking. "I don't know what I'm doing lately, Lexi. I used to have a clear plan; now I feel like I'm flying by the seat of my pants toward I don't know what. It's scary."

"I've been there. That's not a fun feeling, but you don't ever need to be scared, Willa. If you stumble, I'll always be here to help you back onto your feet."

For the first time in a long time Willa felt that she and Lexi were on the same side. Her eyes misted over. This was what she'd missed. She needed to make sure they made amends so they wouldn't lose each other again. "I am so sorry about everything I said—"

"It's no big deal, Willa."

"Yes, it is. You were right to call me out on it. My way isn't the better way. Hell, I don't even know what my way is anymore. You're fearless, while I've always been afraid."

"Fearless? Me? I'm a wreck on the inside. I just don't let it stop me."

Willa took another gulp of her wine. "Every time I try to

be that way I get hurt. Every time. I'm not you."

Lexi reached out and covered Willa's hand with hers. "No, you're not, you're a better person than I am. You're the most honest, loving person I've ever met. You genuinely want the best for everyone you meet. I don't know a single person you don't like. You see good in everyone. I wish I were like that. I wish I could love the way you do."

Willa turned her hand so she was gripping her sister's. "And I wish I had your grit. Your quick wit. When you walk into a room, heads turn because you carry yourself with a confidence impossible not to envy. You can do anything you set your mind to and make it look easy. If something knocks you down, you get up and kick the shit out of it. I wish I had your fight."

"Maybe we both have it wrong—and right. I've spent half of my life trying to change you and the other half wishing I was more like you."

Willa gasped at how perfectly Lexi's words described how she'd felt. "Yes." She wiped a tear from her cheek. "I don't want you to change, Lexi. I need my strong sister."

Lexi's eyes teared up as well. "And I need you." She sniffed loudly and used her napkin to dab at her tears before they ruined her makeup. "We also need to ease up on the wine, or I'm going to be bawling into my sushi, and I do not look good with puffy eyes."

Willa chuckled and released her hand. "We have that in common."

Between bites, Lexi said, "So, tell me how you went from working for Clay to working for Dax. Or skip to the good part, and tell me all about how you ended up hooking up with Lance. Spill."

Closing her hand around her napkin, Willa inwardly confronted a philosophy she'd had for so long it had become part of her identity. She thought if she could push things out of her thoughts, if she could deny them long enough, they would lose the power to hurt her. If that were true she wouldn't be looking across the table at a sister she'd fought to hold on to but somehow ended up alienating anyway.

It was time to borrow some of Lexi's courage. "Lexi, I know you think that pretending to be me with Lance was why we fought that first semester at university."

"It was a stupid thing to do, Willa. I knew you liked him, and I wanted to make sure he was serious about you. I didn't want you to connect with him if he wasn't."

Willa took a deep breath and plowed forward. "I had already slept with him by the time you did that."

Lexi grimaced. "I sort of figured that out on *my date* with him. I didn't expect the kiss, but wham there it was and I *knew*. That's all that ever happened between us, Willa—just that one kiss."

"I believe you." And she did. Lexi had never lied to Willa. If she screwed up, she was the first to say she did and own up to it. It was in the remorse department that she'd sometimes struggled.

Lexi chewed a corner of her acrylic nail. "I tried to tell you that back then, but you wouldn't hear it. I was afraid you'd never forgive me. Then we started school, and instead of getting over it, you got angrier. I didn't know what to do."

"I was pregnant."

"No . . ."

"Yes."

"I would have known."

"I wasn't that far along. I used a home test when I missed my period. I went to the school clinic to confirm it."

Suddenly pale, Lexi looked at a loss for what to say. She opened and closed her mouth a few times but no words came out.

Deciding to go on and get it all out, Willa continued, "I was scared. I didn't know what was going to happen or how it would change my life. Or if I was ready for anything to change. I wanted to tell Lance, but he was angry about the switch. He'd thought I'd asked you to stand in for me. I also couldn't talk to Kenzi."

"And me?"

Willa shrugged a shoulder sadly. "I blamed you. I see now how unfair that was. I wasn't thinking straight. I looked into getting an abortion, but I couldn't do it. I decided to keep the baby even if it meant dropping out of school. It wasn't just any baby, it was Lance's. I was ready to trade it all to have a piece of him in my life."

"That's why you said no to all the parties I invited you to. I thought you didn't want to be with me. But I don't understand. What happened to the baby?"

Blinking back tears, Willa said, "I lost it. You were out with friends when I miscarried."

Lexi blanched. "You could have called me. I would have been there for you." As the news Willa had told her sunk in,

Lexi's face crumpled, and she brought a shaky hand up to her mouth. All bravado fell away and there was only raw remorse in her eyes. "I would have been there for you if I'd known, Willa."

Willa stood up, walked around the table and put her arms around Lexi. "I know that now. At the time I was ashamed. I was the *responsible virgin* in the family. I gave in one time and got pregnant. I didn't want to be pregnant. I didn't know what to do. I didn't want to be someone who would abort a baby, but I didn't see another option at first. I spent weeks torn between telling you or staying silent. I almost called Lance about a thousand times. Everything was so screwed up between all of us, though, that I couldn't. Not that you wouldn't have been there for me, but I couldn't get past what had happened. I didn't think I could handle raising a baby, but the more I thought about it, the more I felt I could make it work. I could love that baby. And I did love it. I wanted the baby. Then I started bleeding in the shower one day and I knew . . . even before the doctors told me what had happened . . . I knew. I can't begin to describe the guilt I felt. Did I wait too long to see a doctor? Was it the drinks I had before I realized I was pregnant? Was it all somehow my fault? I felt that it was. How could I tell anyone how I felt when I had the added guilt of being relieved in a way that my life wouldn't change? But it did change. I'm not the person I was before the baby. I never will be again."

Lexi stood and hugged her back. "I'm an idiot. I don't know how I didn't see it."

"I could have said something, but I wanted to forget. It's

why I couldn't look at Lance without getting upset. Whenever I was with him it brought back all of that. I wanted to put it behind me."

Lexi straightened. "I don't know what else to say except I'm so sorry."

There was a time when Lexi's apology was all Willa wanted, but it now paled in comparison to what was really important. They were finally talking openly, honestly. "I'm not telling you this because I want you to feel badly. I'm trying to say that I'm sorry, too. I tried to rein you in because I was afraid. Mom and Dad followed their adventurous dreams and that decision took them away from us. I followed mine once, and I felt like I lost everything, including my sense of who I was. I didn't want to lose you, too. I thought if I could keep us both on a safe path, I could somehow stop anything tragic from happening. I didn't mean to make you feel that you weren't good enough, Lexi. I never thought that."

Returning to her seat, Willa gulped down the rest of the wine in her glass. Lexi moved closer and said, "I don't let myself care when things go wrong, Willa. I guess that's my way of controlling things. If I don't care, it can't hurt me. I told myself there was nothing I could do to make things better between us because I didn't want to think it could be my fault. If it was, then I'd have to find a way to fix it and face the possibility that I might not be able to."

Willa took her sister's hand in hers. "Even when I was at my lowest, I always loved and appreciated you. You're my best friend. And you always will be."

Lexi gave her hand an equally strong squeeze. "I love you, too." She cleared her throat and in a much lighter tone said, "Can we move on to the important part? Lance? How did that happen?"

Willa chuckled even as she wiped the last trace of tears from her cheeks. "That's your fault. You and that damn flash mob."

"That wasn't actually my idea. Do you remember the dinner party at the Barringtons when Dax brought Clay with him for the first time? He and I were doing shots of tequila while watching you and Lance sneak looks at each other. I don't remember all the details of it, but we got into a debate about life and if anyone actually achieves happiness. He asked me what would make me happy. You know how sappy tequila makes me. I said I wish you and Lance would finally see that you belong together. Clay bet me he could make that happen."

Willa frowned. "Wait, you had me dance for Lance on a bet?"

"Technically, yes." Lexi waved a hand to dismiss that portion. "But the two of you are together now."

"I don't know," Willa said somberly. Over a couple more glasses of wine, she brought her sister completely up to date. She didn't hold anything back. She started with how Dax hadn't seemed to want her to work for Clay. "Oh, my God, I wonder if Dax knew about the bet?"

"Does it matter?" Lexi asked. "It worked."

"I guess it doesn't matter how we got together," Willa said, not completely convinced. "Being with him, Lexi, is so good it's terrifying. I keep waiting for it to end." She told Lexi about the playful way she and Lance had staged a second first meeting. She walked her through the wonder of their craft fair date and how much she'd enjoyed meeting his friends. She told her about touring Emily's museum, being caught by Asher, and his reaction to them dating. Before Lexi had a chance to comment on that, Willa went on to describe how welcoming everyone had been when she'd gone to dinner with the family. She kept the intimate details of Cape Cod to herself but shared how amazing it had been to be with him. Her smile wavered however when she retold how a phone call had stopped her from finally telling him everything and how strained the long ride home had felt. "I know this sounds paranoid, but I don't know if I believe that there was really an emergency at his office. Am I being ridiculous? Why would he lie?"

Lexi wrinkled her nose. "I would tell you to call him, but I'm buzzed. I wouldn't take my own advice right now."

Although Willa didn't feel drunk, she'd definitely had more than her norm. "I can't call him. What would I even say? I can't ask him if he lied to me. Who admits to that?"

"Do you want me to do it?" Lexi asked then quickly added, "Just kidding."

Willa waved a finger. "Not funny. So not funny." But she found herself smiling.

Pouring the last of their second bottle into her glass, Lexi said, "He'll call. He said he would, didn't he?"

Resting her head on one hand, Willa thought back over their parting conversation. "Come to think of it, he didn't say he would."

After a long pause, Willa raised her head slightly. "What did you promise Clay if he won the bet?"

Lexi covered her eyes and groaned. "That's the part of the conversation I can't remember. I'm not too worried about it, though. I don't believe an inebriated bet is a binding agreement. He hasn't mentioned it since, so he might not remember either."

LANCE WENT FOR a long run that night and another one in the morning before heading to his office. He threw himself into working furiously on the Capitol Complex plans for the next few days, hoping to find some clarity in that distraction, but he didn't. All he saw when he looked at his proposal was what it lacked.

He'd redesigned the open space to allow for flow and optimal space, but there was nothing to draw people in. It lacked heart.

Like me.

Willa needs someone who loves her. Why can't I say those words?

I want to be with her. What's holding me back?

He spun his chair so he could stare out the window of his office. Out of the corner of his eye he spotted his aunt's journal sticking out of the corner of his computer bag.

That book, a fucking old woman's ramblings, is somehow the answer—but to which question?

He cleared his desk and retrieved the journal. On a piece of graph paper, he copied the numbers from the pages that led up to where Patrice had torn out pages. Patterns emerged. Some of the numbers repeated in sequence.

Instinctively, he reached for his phone. "Willa, I figured it out."

"What?"

"All the numbers in my aunt's journal. Some are phone numbers, but the rest is a code. Names, addresses. It's a fucking code. I can't believe I didn't see it before."

"What do you think it means?"

"It means I'm going to Aruba."

"So the problem at work is resolved?"

"What problem? Oh, that. I—" *Fuck.* "Willa—"

"There wasn't a problem, was there?"

In the quiet moment that Lance used to choose his next words, Willa hung up.

I told myself I wouldn't hurt her this time. I swore I'd do it the right way.

Why do I keep fucking this up?

That question plagued him for the next two days. He almost called her a hundred times, but stopped when he realized he didn't yet know what to say.

On a whim born in frustration, Lance flew to Aruba and tracked down the first name on the list. It was a doctor. Lance shamelessly bribed the record's clerk at the private hospital where Kenzi and Kent had been born to look up the name. He hadn't delivered the babies, but he'd worked there at the time they were born.

Where was the doctor now?

He died in a car crash that same month.

And the doctor who had delivered Kenzi and Kent?

Dead from a heart attack during the same time period.

Lance went to the address that had been written in code, but no one there knew the name that had been written next to it. Refusing to give up, Lance checked into a hotel and searched through his wallet for the little black card with the white phone number on it. He paced his hotel suite and called it and when he heard someone pick up, he said, "I'm in Aruba."

"Good."

"I found a code in the journal. It's names and addresses."

"I know."

"If you knew, why not say it? Is this some kind of game?"

"Did you locate the people from the list?"

"So far they're all dead." Even as he said the words they sounded unbelievable to him.

"That doesn't sound like a game to me."

Lance rubbed a hand roughly over his forehead. "How much? Name your price. Just tell me what you know."

"Keep your money, Lance. The more I get to know your family, the less I'm sure pushing you was the right decision. Go home."

"Go home? Are you fucking serious?"

"I don't want your death on my conscience."

"*My death?* I don't understand. What happened here?"

"It's bigger than I thought and not worth the risk. Go home." With that, the woman hung up and didn't answer when Lance tried to call her back.

For a few more days, Lance tried to locate the other people on the list. He hired a local private investigator, who tracked down one of the men. He had lived with his sister at the address from the list, but they'd moved away years ago. Twenty-eight years ago.

No one knew where they'd gone or had heard from them since.

They'd simply disappeared.

All during the time his parents were in Aruba. Every answer he found led to more questions.

After another frustrating day without answers, Lance paid the investigator to keep digging and flew back to Boston. He knew he had to tell his brothers what he'd discovered but decided not to until he knew something for sure. Anything.

Even though he'd arrived home late, Lance drove over to Willa's place and called her. She didn't pick up.

His phone beeped with an incoming message. *I don't want to see you.*

He texted back, *I understand why you're not happy with me. I'm an ass. But I'm an ass who is parked out in front of your building, hoping he can make it up to you.*

I don't want you to. Sorry you drove over here for nothing.

And there it is. We've come full circle again. *I'm sorry. More groveling. I shouldn't have lied to you.*

I can't do this, Lance. Being with you can be so good, but then it hurts so bad. Please, just stay away from me for a while.

Lance rested his head on his steering wheel. He felt sick to his stomach and more miserable than he could ever remember feeling. He wanted to rewind to the first time they were together and handle her declaration of love better. He wanted to go back to the previous weekend and not have lost his shit when she'd been about to say it again.

Is this how love feels?

Or am I dying?

On impulse, he did something completely against his family's code. "Dad, do you mind if I drop by? I need to talk to you about something, and it's important."

"Absolutely." The urgency in his father's voice was attributable to the novelty of the request. Barringtons didn't ask each other for advice. No matter how dirty and bloody they got in the trenches of life outside the family, they knew not to bring problems home.

"It'll take me about forty-five minutes to get there." Considering the late hour, he knew he probably should have gone to see him the next day, but he couldn't wait.

"I'll be here," his father said.

After hanging up, he closed his eyes and took a deep breath. His parents might not have the perfect marriage, but they'd stayed together through rough times. There was no question that his father loved his mother and vice versa. Maybe his father could make sense of his son's tangled insides.

When Lance pulled into his parents' driveway he was surprised to see several cars there. Asher's, Grant's, Ian's and, if Lance wasn't mistaken, Dax's.

Shit.

The door flew open. With slightly mussed hair as if she'd gone to bed then gotten dressed again after his call, his mother stood in the doorway and beckoned him in. "I heard your father telling Asher to come over quickly, and I was worried. What's wrong, Lance?"

A lifetime of training had Lance automatically answering, "Nothing, Mom."

Sophie closed the door behind her. It was opened a second later by a concerned looking Dale. Sophie waved him away and said, "Give us a moment alone, please."

Dale reluctantly closed the door again.

Sophie moved to sit on the top step and said, "Sit with me, Lance."

Lance took a seat beside her. This was uncharted territory for him. "I didn't mean to wake everyone up. I should have waited until tomorrow."

Placing her hand on Lance's arm, his mother said, "You're exactly where you belong. Especially if something is troubling you."

"It's nothing important."

Sophie sighed and her hand dropped. "I used to think I was a good mother—"

"You are—"

"Let me say this. My mother died in childbirth having me. I never knew her. I don't know if my father ever forgave my sister or me for that. People say he wasn't the same after she died. I don't know because all I knew was the man who looked through me instead of at me. No matter what my sister or I did, it was never good enough. He might have wanted to love us, but we knew he didn't. I moved away from my family because I wanted my own children to be raised differently. I wanted you to always know exactly how much you were loved." She blinked back tears. "After we lost Kent, I fell into a depression. It was rough on all of you. Especially your father. He wanted to fix everything that was wrong, but sometimes you can't. So he tried to give me the perfect family he thought I needed. Kenzi opened your father's and my eyes to what we've done well and where we've failed you."

"Mom, I don't know what Kenzi said, but you didn't fail anyone."

Sophie squeezed Lance's forearm with one hand. "I'm not perfect, Lance—far from it. Your father isn't either, and that's okay. Love isn't about never being wrong. It's taking the best and the worst of who we are and knowing that we're better together than we could ever be apart. I'm not as fragile as everyone thinks I am. You can get angry with me. You can disappoint me. I'll still love you. Whatever problem you're wrestling with, Lance, you can bring it to my door—night or day, and I will always want to hear it. Because you're my son. And that bond is stronger than anything life can throw at us."

Hearing his mother's description of love was freeing. Lance had grown up thinking of love as something so delicate it might shatter from the slightest application of pressure just like his mother. Yet, there she was, facing her mistakes and the reality that her children weren't as happy as they pretended to be, and she wasn't falling to pieces.

Maybe love was a little more resilient than he gave it credit for.

He sat quietly beside his mother for several long moments. Then he said, "I think I love Willa."

With a gentle smile, Sophie asked, "You think? Not sure?"

Lance raised and dropped a shoulder. "She's perfect for me. I am happier when I'm with her than I've ever been without her. And I'm more miserable when we're apart than I can put into words. We've only really started dating, and I've already said stupid things and hurt her again. Probably the best thing for her would be if I stayed away from her, but I can't seem to."

"Love by definition is scary as hell. Do you know why?"

Lance shook his head.

"It's an all or nothing decision. You have to believe in it to fully feel it. It not only requires that you give yourself over to it, but if you don't trust it, it withers like a plant without water. You can't think you love someone, Lance. You have to know it. Imagine your life without Willa in it. If you can do that, and see yourself happy without her . . . walk away. But if the idea of being without her tears you up inside—if you would gladly trade everything you have for one more day with her—then she's the one for you."

Lance thought about his friend Neil and how much he regretted losing Linda.

I'd be a hundred times worse.

I don't want to go a day without Willa.

Lance leaned over and kissed his mother on the cheek. "I love her, Mom. I love Willa Chambers."

Sophie smiled. "I know you do."

"I need to tell her."

His mother glanced down at her watch. "Maybe not at this time of night. Everyone is here. Why not come in and at least say hello? Your father dragged them all here for an emergency family meeting. Poor Dax, I don't know what he was expecting, but he came. Kenzi, too. Emily is home resting."

Lance stood and helped his mother up. "They're going to kill me."

Sophie linked her arm through his. "Not on my watch."

Lance chuckled. He'd never imagined his mother as plucky as she sounded. "I like this side of you, Mom."

"I do, too. Come on. Let's go inside, and we can plan out how you should propose to my next daughter."

Propose?

He waited for the panic to come, but it didn't.

He pictured coming home to Willa. Waking with her in his arms. A flash forward in time would have them visiting his parents with their children in tow.

There were many things he didn't know, many questions he couldn't answer, but how he felt about Willa was no longer one of them.

Chapter Seventeen

>>>><<<<

WILLA WIPED HER hands on a towel and sat back to study her creation. At Emily's suggestion, she'd spent every night that week working on a piece for Emily's museum. It was a welcome distraction from what was otherwise turning out to be another miserable week.

I knew it would hurt when it ended, but I didn't expect it to end so soon. Or so abruptly.

Or for him to lie.

Although Willa had started off thinking she would paint something, she'd turned to working with clay as a way to vent some of her frustration. Last week she'd worried that Lance was actually dealing with a crisis at work, but now she knew the truth.

Sex doesn't mean the same thing to men that it does to women. We had a good time together, but that's it. I just wish he'd had the balls to tell me he only wanted one night.

My heart would be just as broken, but at least I wouldn't have run to my cell phone every time it rang like some idiot. I wouldn't have opened my heart so freely to him.

Or maybe I would have.

It's always been all or nothing with Lance.
When will I learn?

What wasn't helping her forget him was the damn bouquet of flowers she still received from him daily. They always came with a note she refused to read. She didn't want another apology from him. *I want to stick those flowers up his ass.*

He only pretends to care about me until I fall for it. Then BAM—every time.

As her mood darkened, Willa forced herself to go back to working on the clay sculpture. *Maybe the flowers need to keep coming so I'll remember what an ass he is.*

He doesn't define me.

She sat back and studied the piece she was working on. She'd chosen her relationship with her sister as the subject. Two identical figurines stood on either side of a double-sided full-length mirror, holding hands by reaching around it. Their reflection was a painting of their soul rather than their actual stance. On Lexi's side, Willa had portrayed her sister as a warrior in her reflection with one hand placed defiantly on her hip, but she'd softened the image by making her eyes thoughtful, as if she had secrets that gave her great depth.

It was her depiction of herself in the mirror that Willa had struggled with. Her first attempt had been to show herself as trapped and afraid, but Willa realized that was no longer who she was. The feelings of abandonment that stemmed from when she was younger were still present, but they no longer ruled her.

So who am I?

Not a warrior.

Not a victim.

Willa worked the image in the mirror until she captured what she hoped represented herself. The lines of her face were soft, but her chin was set at a proud angle. Down her chest, she made a scar that hinted at a near-deadly wound that had healed over. The woman in the mirror wasn't ashamed of her scar.

I'm that woman. Not perfect, but beautiful nonetheless. Scarred, but proud.

She dropped her hands from the sculpture again. *And I'm a survivor. I don't need Lance to be okay. He hurt me, but he didn't break me.* She went back to her image of herself in the mirror and tweaked the expression in the woman's eyes. *I'm in love with a man who doesn't love me, but there is beauty in that. My ability to love and forgive is my strength, not my weakness.*

Her cell phone rang. Since her hands were covered with clay, she didn't answer it, but she checked the caller ID.

Lance.

A text came in a moment later. **Call me.**

Willa shook her head and walked away from the phone. Her emotions were flying in all directions as she went back to working on her piece.

Call me?

Really?

If he wants me to so much as look at him again, he'll have to do a hell of a lot better than that.

BACK IN HIS office, Lance stood and stretched after answering the last of his morning emails. He checked his phone for a response from Willa but found none. She still wasn't taking his calls, acknowledging his flowers, or answering his texts. Lance wasn't worried, though. He had a plan.

He walked over to his office window and looked at the skyline as his thoughts flew back to his parents' house the night before. He'd walked in with his mother on his arm and been greeted by almost every member of his immediate family. Asher, Ian, and Grant had stood beside Dale like a small army preparing for battle. Kenzi stood beside Dax, part of the group but off to one side.

Dale looked back and forth between his wife and his youngest son. "Is everything all right?"

Sophie had nodded and said, "Why don't we all go into the living room and sit while we talk?"

She led the way and soon they were all gathered around where she and Lance were seated. "Lance why don't you tell them what you discovered?"

Asher was the first to speak. "Dad said you're in trouble. What's going on, Lance?"

"If it's financial, I could look over your books and come up with a plan," Grant said.

Ever the problem solver, Ian said, "If it's illegal, don't say anything to anyone. Except us. Knowing exactly what you did will help us choose the best lawyer."

Dax stood near the door, arms folded across his chest. Present, but silent.

Dale followed Lance's gaze and said, "Whatever issues

you two boys have, it doesn't matter. We all need to support each other."

It was what his father had always said, but they were just words. The unstated expectation that they should deal with things on their own had made that sentiment unnecessary.

With a nod, Dax confirmed his support, which was interesting since he didn't have any idea why he'd been called there. His presence was a testament to his loyalty to the Barringtons.

And to me.

"Thanks for coming, Dax." He looked around at his brothers. "Thank you all for coming, but I'm not in any kind of trouble."

"Bull," Asher said harshly. "Something's wrong. You look like shit."

Giving Lance another once-over, Ian asked, "Are you on drugs?"

Their mother shook her head in reprimand. "Really, Ian? Must you always think the worst? Let him speak."

Lance shook his head. "Of course I'm not on drugs."

"Are you sick?" Grant asked looking genuinely concerned that he might be.

"No."

"Is guilt keeping you up at night?" Dax asked gruffly. All eyes turned to toward Dax and he shrugged. "Willa's not having a good week either. You know why, don't you?"

"Yes," Lance said abruptly. It wasn't easy to hear that Willa was unhappy and he was the cause, but he was about to change that. He liked Dax even more for the way he came to Willa's defense.

He's loyal to her, too.

You chose well, Kenzi.

"This is about Willa?" Ian asked incredulously. "I thought the two of you were dating now."

"We are. We were. I messed up," Lance answered.

"I can't believe you called us here for this," Asher said to Dale.

Dale gave Asher an authoritative look that always put him back a step. "Sit down, Asher. In fact, why don't we all? Lance obviously wants our help."

Grant rubbed a hand on the back of his neck. "I don't know what you expect us to do, Dad. This is between him and Willa."

"Sit," Dale said.

The Barrington men sat down in the couches and chairs around where Sophie and Lance sat. Kenzi encouraged Dax to sit with them.

Asher nodded at the open love seat beside him, "Get your ass over here, Dax. You wanted to be one of us. Welcome to the Twilight Zone."

Once everyone was seated, Sophie said, "Lance has had an epiphany."

Lance stood up and began to pace. The entire scene was over the top, but he thought back to the night Dax had asked the family to help him plan his proposal to Kenzi. Lance had learned early that Barringtons handled their own problems, but maybe, just maybe, that was changing. He wanted his family to feel as invested in Willa's acceptance as they had in Kenzi's. "I'm in love with Willa."

Asher's phone rang. "It's Emily," he said to no one in particular before answering it. "He's fine. Everyone is fine. Lance has temporarily lost his mind, though. The emergency was he wanted to tell us that he loves Willa." Asher listened to whatever his wife was saying, then responded. "I know you knew that. We all knew it. The only one surprised seems to be Lance." He listened again, then pressed a button on his phone and held it up. "Okay, you're on video chat now."

Emily waved from the screen of the phone. "Lance, I'm so sorry I couldn't be there. The doctor told me to try to get more rest. You must be over-the-moon happy."

Not yet. "Technically, she's still not speaking to me. That's why I'm here. I messed things up with her the first time. I'm very close to losing her a second time. I needed some advice so I came to see Dad, but Mom is also a good sounding board."

Dale crossed to stand behind his wife. He bent down and kissed her cheek. She raised a hand to hold his. "When it comes to love, you spoke to the expert."

Sophie smiled and squeezed her husband's hand. "A good marriage takes two. You and I have made our share of mistakes, but I hope we've shown our children that love and family can survive anything. I love you more today, Dale, than I did when I agreed to marry you—and I was head-over-heels smitten with you then. More than anything else, that's what I want for our children. I want them to find someone who stands with them no matter what challenges their bond."

Dale's eyes shone with emotion. "I would do it again, Sophie. Every last moment. The good. The bad. It was all worth it because you were at my side." He looked around the room. "As I watch our children growing up and starting families of their own, I hope they do a hundred things better than we did, but one thing the same. I hope they always end each day grateful to have each other. Every one of us in this room has done something we regret, but if we work through it, we become stronger because of it."

For the second time that night Lance's perception of his parents was challenged. Yes, their marriage had its flaws, yet its foundation was not only solid but had strengthened over time. That's what he wanted for himself and Willa.

From the phone, Emily said, "Am I the only one bawling?"

Kenzi called out, "I'm right there with you."

Grant cleared his throat. "So, what are we doing now?"

"Hang on a minute." Lance walked out of the living room into his father's office and returned with a white board and dry erase marker. In much the same fashion that he'd outline a timetable for work projects—with lines that jutted out to boxes where he listed possible complications along with solutions to each—he charted his relationship with Willa. He kept the details to a minimum referring only to their intimacy as the times they connected.

He stood back, studied the diagram and said, "As you can see, I need a clear plan of action to break this pattern."

Dax said, "That's quite a chart you have there, Lance."

Ian studied the details of it. "Why is Lexi in a box with

an asterisk?"

"That's when she pretended to be Willa, and I didn't realize it."

"Tell me you didn't sleep with her sister," Asher said abruptly.

Sophie gasped. Dale's eyes flew to Lance's but he didn't say anything.

Lance erased the asterisk. "One kiss, but it was enough to screw everything up the first time."

Dax rubbed a finger and thumb over his eyes before looking up at the chart. "This is how you think? You're not making this up?"

Lance shrugged. "I can't wing it this time. I need to look at this problem from all angles." He added a mathematical equation that he'd toyed with mid-week. "This is my calculation of the length of time it'll take her to forgive me for not calling her this week. I based it on how long she was angry the first time, then factored in the similarities and differences between each event. I think we should figure out this portion before I move on to the proposal."

Dax looked around at the other men as if gauging the likelihood that one of them would announce he was being pranked. When there was no confirmation, Dax turned his attention back to Lance. "You're serious about all of this?"

Kenzi laid her head on his arm. "He loves her. Don't even pretend it wasn't confusing for you when you realized you loved me."

There was a general chuckle around the room.

Lance lowered the dry erase board and sat heavily on the

arm of one of the couches. "Laugh all you want, but I can't lose her again. I've been in love with her for a long time. I just couldn't see it."

Ian said, "I don't know how you missed it when it was clearly there in the subcategory of your third bulleted list of reasons you belonged together."

Lance glanced down at his diagram, shocked he'd missed that, only to realize that his brother had made it up.

"Ian," Dale said, using his son's name in reprimand.

Waving his hands in the air, Ian defended himself. "Dad, what do you expect? This is ridiculous."

With a shake of his head, Dale said, "Love humbles a man, Ian, especially while you're working things out the way Lance is. Ask Asher and Dax."

"I could have used a diagram when I was trying to figure out if I'd burned Emily's museum down," Asher said with self-deprecating humor.

Emily chimed in. "That was not a fun time for any of us. I thought it might be over between us right up until the moment you proposed."

"Falling in love is hell," Dax confirmed.

Kenzi raised her head and her eyebrows shot to her hairline.

He smiled and gave her a brief kiss on the lips. "But then, if you survive the wedding planning, it's all good."

With a playful elbow nudge, Kenzi said, "You wait. You'll pay for that one."

The couple was momentarily lost in each other's eyes. Lance and everyone else looked away. Lance circled back to his problem. "I screwed up. She was about to tell me she loved me, and I bolted. Then I didn't call her. Now she's not answering my calls."

"Oh, Lance," Kenzi said. "No wonder she's been avoiding me."

Emily added, "She's been working on a sculpture at my museum every night. You should see it. It's incredible."

"Have you thought about hiring her to cover for you when you're on maternity leave?" Dax asked.

Sophie tipped her head in question. "She's not working at your office?"

Lance found it amusing to watch Dax weigh being honest with pleasing his future mother-in-law. "She's an artist at heart. She'd be happier in a museum setting."

"Good save," Ian interjected softly.

Lance turned and erased the board then picked up the marker again. Dax's suggestion had given him an idea. "Proposing is the next logical step. And the way I see it, there are only a couple of viable places I should ask her. But first I have to get her there. While you're all here . . ."

There were a few groans from around the room, but no one moved to leave. He started listing places he knew Willa loved and adding pros and cons next to each. He also added the idea of showing her in some concrete fashion how important she was to him.

Reminiscent of how his family was when they played Pictionary together, everyone started calling out suggestions. Lance paused before writing down each idea and looked around at those gathered for the single purpose of helping him. *My family. This is what my friends imagine I have when I tell them I'm from a large family. Asher bringing Emily home changed us, woke us up. Maybe things won't go back to how they were before. Maybe good things really can last.* It gave him hope, not only within his family, but within himself.

And with Willa.

He knew that one day soon he'd have to discuss what he'd discovered in Aruba, but he wanted Willa at his side when he did. His father wanted them to do things better than he had. Lance wanted to share his life with Willa—the best and the worst of whatever was to come. Together, they could weather any storm.

Family and love.

It had taken him a long time, but he finally believed in both, and with his family's help, he'd convince Willa to do the same.

Chapter Eighteen

>>><<<

A FEW DAYS later after the museum was closed, Willa and Lexi walked into the Harris Tactile Museum. After checking in with a staff member, Willa asked Lexi to don a blindfold. Her sculpture was finished and on display in the main hallway. Willa wanted her sister to experience it first through touch.

Lexi laughed, put the blindfold on, then held her arm out for her sister to take. "Lead away. When you said you were embracing your artistic side, I had no idea how serious you were. I can't wait to see—I mean feel what you made. It must be good if Emily is letting you showcase it."

Emily's reaction had been incredible. Yes, she cried, but . . . she was very pregnant. She cried easily. Her words, though, would ring within Willa forever. "Stunning, Willa. It's breathtaking," Willa had nearly fallen in shock.

Willa led her sister by the arm. "I hope you like it as much as she did. Having it included among Emily's pieces and her mother's makes my decision to work here that much more exciting. When I'm in this building I feel like I'm an artist."

"You are one. You always have been."

Willa hugged her sister's arm. "In my heart, maybe, but I didn't have the confidence to create anything. Don't expect the sculpture to feel perfectly formed. It has some rough spots where I struggled to get it right, but it's a piece of me, and Emily says that's what makes it beautiful."

Stopping within inches of her sculpture, Willa placed Lexi's hands on one of the figures. Lexi explored it then said, "Is it you? I love it."

Willa's heart pounded joyfully as her sister seemed to genuinely appreciate the work. "Touch what she's looking at."

Lexi ran her hand down the surface across from her and traced the raised image on it. "Is it a mirror?"

"Yes. I tried to raise the outline of it so it would be three dimensional. What do you feel?"

"It's you, but it's different. So this is how you see yourself?" She felt the scar and followed it down the front of the image then moved back up to the expression on the woman's face. "Yes, that's perfect. You should be proud of who you are. You're beautiful, scars and all."

"Now follow her hand."

Lexi returned her touch to the figure and traced her arm down to her hand. She smiled as she explored how it was clasping another hand. She followed the other arm up to that figure's face. "That's me on the other side of the mirror."

"Yes."

Lexi ran her hands over both the figure on the other side and its reflection in the mirror. Her voice thickened with emotion. "I don't know that I'm quite as strong as you think I am, but I try."

Lexi's instant understanding of what Willa had tried to capture, along with her willingness to experience it, gave Willa happy goosebumps. *We're back.*

Willa removed Lexi's blindfold. "You are every bit as beautiful and strong. If you ever doubt that, look at this. Look at us and know how much I love you and value you in my life."

Lexi took a moment to appreciate the combination of painting and sculpture then wiped away a tear and hugged Willa. "I don't know what to say. This is so beautiful."

"Just tell me you love it," Willa said softly. Her sister's opinion mattered. It always had and it always would.

"Now I know where you've been hiding lately. I thought maybe you were hooking up with someone again and didn't want to tell me."

Willa hugged her sister back. "We're beyond that." As she said the words she realized how much she meant them. Lexi had never meant to hurt her and had simply tried to fix the situation. The past had no hold over them anymore. "Besides, I'm taking a break from relationships for a while."

"Have you talked to Lance at all?"

Willa stepped back and shook her head. "Not since I asked him to stop sending flowers, which he still does—every day—and the bouquets keep getting bigger and bigger. It makes it hard to move on."

Lexi pressed her lips together briefly then said, "Do you have to move on? Have you considered picking up the phone and letting him explain?"

Willa clasped her hands in front of her. *I thought she understood. It hurts too much.* "He doesn't need to. I know him. He got scared. We have a chemistry that makes both of us stupid when we're together, but we also have a pattern I don't want to go through again. I hand him my heart on a platter, and *he* runs for the hills. He did it ten years ago. He did it again at Cape Cod. When I'm with him I don't care about the future or if he'll leave me. All I care about is how good it feels. But when he leaves me, it hurts so much. I can't do it again. I can't put myself through that kind of pain again."

Lexi sighed audibly. "I hear that and completely understand. We're good right now—you and I?"

"Absolutely."

"If I ever screw up again, you'll forgive me, right?"

"What did you do, Lexi?"

"Nothing. Just remember that I love you."

Don't panic. She has *learned her lesson. She wouldn't get involved again.* "Please tell me you're not planning to *help* me with something. Everything is fine. Work. My life. Don't do anything."

"It's not *me*." She waved a hand in air while looking a little offended. "Kenzi asked if we could fly down to Florida to check out some wedding sites with her and Dax. I told her we would."

Willa let out a sigh of relief. "That's it?"

Lexi shrugged. "I should have asked you before saying you'd go. Kenzi mentioned you weren't returning her calls. I know you've had a lot on your mind lately, but this will be good for us. We've always said we'd go to Florida together. Now we will."

A memory of their parents promising to take them on a Florida vacation went through Willa's mind. She gripped Lexi's hand. "Let's go to Disney while we're there. It'll be amazing. A dream come true."

"Let's hope it lives up to expectations," Lexi said vaguely. Then smiled. "So, you're in?"

"I'm in," Willa said and thought of something else. "Are you up to the flight?"

"For something like this, I guess I have to be. Besides, we'll be in Dax's private plane. I'm sure they serve martinis." Lexi studied Willa's face for a moment then asked, "You do want to go, don't you?"

"Of course." Willa did, but she couldn't help but think about the last person she'd spoken to about that trip. *Lance.* Willa was relieved to be in a good place with her sister again—and excited they would finally take the trip they'd talked so much about as children—but a part of her wished she could share it with Lance.

Stop.
He's not part my life.
Not anymore.
And I'm okay.
Kind of.

IN A COURTYARD of Disney World's Grand Floridian Resort, Lance paced back and forth. He double-checked that the two-carat engagement ring was still in his suit breast pocket. *Thank God. It is there. At least I didn't screw that part up.* He took a deep calming breath. The actual proposal wasn't what he was having second thoughts about, but rather the delivery.

After the discussion with his family, he'd decided to ask Willa to marry him in a place she'd told him she'd always wanted to go. He'd felt it was important to bring Lexi. Willa's dream had been to go to Disney with her, so he wanted to make that happen. He also wanted them to move forward together. First, Willa's dream. Next, helping Willa heal her family.

My family.

After he married Willa, Lexi would be family.

I hope I don't fuck this up.

No, Lance was certain he'd chosen the right venue.

What he questioned was his decision to tell "Uncle" Alessandro about his plans. Asher had said they'd truly appreciated being there when he'd proposed to Emily, so Lance knew it would be a kind gesture to invite them to this too.

Two people became fifty. Fifty became one hundred. Lance had imagined a simple event. *Simple. Small.* Now it included a ballroom full of guests, a Cinderella-style horse-drawn coach Alessandro had commissioned—despite Lance's protests—a patio where, if everything went perfectly, he would propose... while fireworks went off in the background. *Not simple.*

Alessandro Andrade had most of his family with him and

what appeared to be every child in the New York area. They were well dressed but running wild on the lawns and taking turns going around the property in Cinderella's coach.

Lance's father came to stand beside him. "I'm glad you invited the Andrades. Your mother has grown closer to them this past year. She's always felt she didn't have family beyond us, but her sister's children adore her. This was good."

"It's not quite how I imagined it," Lance said, loosening his tie with one finger. "I hope it's not too much."

"The coach might be," Dale said with a smile. "None of this matters or will determine her answer." He tapped his son's chest. "What's in here will. Tell her you love her. Willa's no stranger to loss. She needs to know you're in this for the long haul. No matter what. Don't do this if there is any question in your heart if she's the one for you. But if you know she is, let yourself enjoy this. Today is a day you'll describe to your children, and God willing, your children's children. Make it a good story."

Lance looked around with fresh eyes. Every single person there, all one hundred of them, had come to celebrate Willa being asked to join his family. He smiled.

Alessandro came over to join them. "The waiting is the hardest part, no?" He shook hands with Dale and then Lance.

Lance nodded. His stomach was still doing flips. "I hope she says yes."

Alessandro clapped a hand on his back. "Don't worry, if she says no, we'll do this again and again until she changes her mind."

Dale laughed. "He's serious."

With a carefree shrug, Alessandro said, "The secret to a lasting marriage is to not give up on each other no matter what." He snapped his fingers. "And always please her first." He smiled. "Forget that and you'll be down the hall wondering how you got your own bedroom."

Lance exchanged a look with his father then burst out laughing, and his nervousness fell away. "I feel prepared for marriage now. Thank you, Alessandro."

"Uncle Alessandro," the old Italian man corrected with a huge smile.

Nodding, Lance repeated, "Uncle Alessandro."

Sophie appeared at Dale's elbow. "They're here. Kenzi texted that they're parking now. Don't forget to call Asher so he and Emily won't miss this. I tried to call Andrew, but he's not available. This is so exciting."

Lance turned to Alessandro and said, "I love that you're all here. I promise I'll introduce Willa to all of you, but I need to talk to her alone first."

"Asher did it his own way, too," Alessandro answered then shrugged. "But it worked out for him. So, yes, go have your talk first. Then the *Grand Gesture*."

Not sure what the hell his "uncle" was talking about, Lance agreed simply to appease him.

Dale put a hand on Lance's shoulder. "Good luck."

Sophie stepped forward and hugged Lance. "He doesn't need luck. We all know she loves him. Now get out there and get me another daughter."

Lance stepped back and chuckled at his mother's playful

demand. *Playful.* She was happy finally, and he felt a sense of ease seeing his mother healing along with the rest of them. "I will."

Chapter Nineteen

BRIDEZILLA KENZI WAS taking Florida by storm. Her tour of potential wedding sites had not only started in Tampa and extended to Orlando but Kenzi also requested all four of them wear formal attire for their food tasting at the Grand Floridian. Willa hadn't brought anything Kenzi had considered up to par, so the trip had also included a quick shopping spree—thankfully on Kenzi's card.

Willa didn't feel the need be to dressed in an expensive gown to help decide if the cake at the Grand Floridian was better than the cake at Clay's Beachside Hotel. But it was important to Kenzi that everything be perfect, so Willa obliged her friend.

Lexi had been unusually quiet all day, but Willa attributed that to residual nervousness from the flight. Dax didn't seem at all worried that his bride-to-be was already going a little over the top.

As they stepped out of their limo—Kenzi's choice of vehicle, of course—Willa wondered if there was a wedding here today. So many cars. "It looks like there's a wedding here today. I wonder what they're like here." She spotted something white in the distance that was coming closer and exclaimed. "Oh my God, is that Cinderella's coach? How cool is that? Is it full of kids? It can't be." As it came closer Willa gasped. It was full of kids. Happy, cheering children. "Now that is fun." She turned to Lexi. "Disney is just as magical as Mom described it. Remember? She used to tell us that this was where happily-ever-afters were born." Willa sighed. Seeing such wonder, she struggled against the disappointment and yearning she felt for her own *happily ever after*.

Not everyone gets a happy ending.

That's why we pay to come to places like this where we can experience what it would be like—even if for a moment.

Willa gave herself a mental shake. This was about Kenzi, so she quickly squashed her feelings. "This place..." She pushed back her disappointment in her own love life and focused on Kenzi's. "This place has my vote, Kenzi. Even before we taste the food."

Kenzi's smile widened. "If you like this, you'll love what comes next."

Lexi, Kenzi, Dax, and Willa walked toward the entrance of a large building that housed several ballrooms. The door to the building opened and Lance stepped out. He didn't stop until he was standing directly in front of Willa. "Hi, Willa."

She swayed and took a step back. "Lance. I didn't know you were meeting us."

Kenzi, Dax, and Lexi excused themselves and headed inside the building. Willa almost bolted to go with them, but

Lance blocked her escape. "I was an idiot in Cape Cod."

Willa raised her hand. "Please. We don't need to rehash this."

Lance took her hand in his and held it even though she tried to pull it free. "We do because I need to explain. I thought you were about to tell me that you loved me, and I didn't want you to."

A cold swept through Willa. "Let go of my hand."

Lance didn't. He grimaced. "That came out wrong. Let me start over."

"Please don't."

"I love you. I've loved you most of my life, but it took me until now to be able to say it."

Willa's legs wobbled beneath her. She wanted desperately to believe that she'd heard what she thought she'd heard, but she was afraid to. "I'm sorry?"

Lance dug in his coat pocket. "I love you. I can't imagine my life without you in it." He dropped to one knee. "Marry me, Willa. I'm a work in progress. My whole family is. I know that. But we need you. I need you."

Willa shook her head as she tried to make sense of the sudden shift in Lance. "You really hurt me."

"I'll spend the rest of my life making it up to you."

Although a part of her wanted to cry, "Yes. Yes. Yes." Another part of her was still recovering from the last time she'd believed in him. "I don't know, Lance."

Lance rose back to his feet and took both of her hands in his. "I do. I didn't before and I'm sorry, but I know now. We belong together."

"You didn't call me at all after Cape Cod. Nothing. Not for a week. Why?"

Lance's expression was contrite. "I went to Aruba. I wish I could say that was the only reason, but I also needed to sort out how I felt about you."

Willa swallowed hard, keeping a part of her heart protected. "And you've done that now?"

"Yes."

"I don't know if I believe you, Lance. I want to, but I don't know if I can."

Lance blanched. "I deserve that. I should have let you say it that night, Willa. I was just so afraid I wouldn't say the right thing and I'd lose you again."

What Willa had held in for so long came rushing forward, and she knew she couldn't say yes or no to him until she told him the truth. "I wasn't going to say I loved you that day. What I needed to say was about what happened after that summer night ten years ago. After we were together." She closed her eyes briefly for strength, then opened them and plowed forward. "I was pregnant, Lance. Pregnant with your baby, but I was too afraid to tell you. I considered all possibilities, even abortion, then finally decided to keep it." Her eyes blurred with tears. "But I miscarried. I lost our baby, and it was like losing you all over again. It nearly destroyed me."

Lanced cradled her to his chest, shattered by the news. "Willa, I don't know what to say. I had no idea."

Willa breathed in the scent of him, not sure if she would ever be so close to him again. "I know you didn't. No one did."

He released his hold and raised her head by placing a finger beneath her chin. Looking in her eyes, he said, "I was young. I was stupid, but I would have been there for you. You have to know that. I am so sorry you went through that alone. I would do anything to be able to go back and shoulder that pain for you, or to stand with you as you went through it. I should have checked on you. I knew the condom broke. It's my fault you were alone through that. I let you down. No wonder you couldn't look at me. I should have been there for you, Willa. Give me a chance, and I'll be there now and every time you need me from this moment on. I swear to you I will."

Willa searched his face and the love she saw in his misty eyes melted away the wall she'd erected to protect her heart. She'd known him for over twelve years, and he wasn't one to lie. He hid his heart, but he was a good man. She understood what others would have seen as his flaws. It was habitual, instinctive for him to pretend, hiding away his true emotions. But . . . he wasn't hiding his feelings from her. He meant every word he'd said. The truth was in his eyes. He looked as devastated now as she had felt when she knew she was losing the baby. She reminded herself of what she'd acknowledged in her sculpture. *I don't need Lance to be okay. I am stronger than anything that can happen to me or anyone who can leave me. I'm not more or less than Lexi. I'm simply Me. And, I don't have to hide anymore. I may be afraid, but my fears will no longer rule me. I won't throw away this chance of happiness because it can be torn away from me. My ability to love and forgive is my strength, not my weakness.*

His face contorted with pain and he didn't hide the tear that spilled over. "I would do anything to be able to go back and be the man you thought I was. I should have been at your side through everything. I will be from now on, Willa. I love you."

He loves me.

Believing him, believing in him is my choice. I could walk away and protect my heart, or I can take this leap of faith.

I choose him.

She would always feel the loss, but now she wasn't alone *in* that loss. "I love you, Lance Barrington." *I always have.* "Lance, I do love you."

He laid his forehead on hers. "Does that mean you'll marry me?"

"My head is spinning. I need a minute." Things with Lance were always full speed, and she simply needed to take a breath before agreeing.

Lance took a piece of paper out of his pocket. It was a design for the City Complex. In the middle of it was a spot circled with her name written on it. "I knew there was something missing in my designs and my life, Willa. It was you. I want you to be part of this project. You can choose what the centerpiece of the complex will be or you can design it yourself."

"You want me to be part of your project?"

"I want to share this and every other part of my life with you. All you have to do is say yes. Yes to me. Yes to my crazy family." He glanced over his shoulder at the building behind them. "I'd like to apologize ahead of time for what's in there."

Willa looked past him. "What's in there? Isn't it just the food tasting?"

Lance chuckled and pocketed the paper. "You wish. My immediate, as well as my extended family is all in there waiting for us. At least a hundred of them."

"One hundred? Here? For us? Why?"

Lance held out the engagement ring again. "Because I told them you're the woman I want to spend the rest of my life with."

Willa swayed again, but happily this time. *I'm not imagining this. He loves me, and this is real.* "Were you that sure I'd say yes? What if I said no?"

"I would have asked you again. And my family would have gathered for that, too. They love you." Lance's expression changed and his eyes filled with desire. "My uncle gave me advice on how to keep a marriage happy."

"Did he?" Willa asked. She'd already decided she'd say yes to Lance, but after the week he'd put her through, she didn't mind making him sweat for a little bit.

Lance bent and whispered *Uncle* Allesandro's advice in Willa's ear. A flush of desire rocketed through her. *That's real, too.* "I like that."

The Cinderella coach pulled up to the curb beside Lance and Willa. Several children and one adult exited. The driver asked if Lance and Willa would like a ride.

Willa looked up at Lance. "Would it be overly corny if I asked you to ask me again as we rode in that coach?"

Lance smiled. "I'll ask you a hundred more times if this day ends with you saying yes."

Willa stepped up into the coach and settled beside Lance. She took his hand in hers and couldn't help but feel her parents were with her just then. "It won't take a hundred. Just once more."

As they rode down a side road, fireworks began to go off in the background, but Willa didn't turn to look at them. She didn't care about anything past Lance and the love he was no longer afraid to express.

"Willa Chambers," Lance asked as he took her hand in his and held the engagement ring out near her left hand, "will you marry me?"

"I will," Willa said as happy tears streamed down her cheeks. "I damn sure will."

Lance slid the ring on her finger and pulled her into a deep kiss. The kind of kiss that was worthy of the fairy-tale setting.

Chapter Twenty

SEVERAL MONTHS LATER, Lance guided Willa into a room of the house they'd purchased together. His hands were over her eyes. "If it's not perfect we can change any part of it you'd like."

"I'm sure I'll love it."

Lance removed his hands and watched his fiancée's expression closely.

She was silent for a long moment, then she turned and flung herself in his arms. "It's perfect. It's exactly as I always imagined it would be."

Lance puffed with pride and hugged her closer. He'd meticulously planned every detail of the library from the rolling ladder to the chairs he imagined Willa would enjoy curling up in while she read. "With this last renovation completed, we can move in."

"Maybe, not just yet," Willa said with an odd smile. "You need to plan out one more room."

"I do?" Lance didn't think he'd missed a single room during the renovations.

"We're going to need a baby room," she said. "We're

having twins."

Lance's jaw dropped as her words sunk in then his hands went to her stomach in wonder. "Twins? How long have you known? Why didn't you say anything?" *I'm going to be a father.* Lance hadn't thought he could be happier, but the idea of Willa having his baby . . . his babies . . . filled him with undeniable warmth and put a huge, stupid smile on his face."

She nodded. "I wanted to wait until—until I was sure. Plus, Emily was still pregnant. I wanted to hold off our announcement until she had Jamus."

Twins. "We're having twins."

Willa laughed. "We are."

Lance frowned. "We need to get married."

"We are getting married."

"I mean now. Right now."

Still chuckling, Willa said, "What about the big wedding your mother was planning?"

"One phone call and we can have all that ready by next weekend."

"You're crazy. Kenzi's wedding should come before ours."

Lance smiled unapologetically. "Trust me, no one will mind." He cupped her slightly rounded stomach. "Twins. We're in trouble."

Willa wrapped her arms around Lance and hugged him tightly. "Yes, but we're in it together."

He kissed her deeply. "We sure are. We took the long

way home, but we got here."

Willa snuggled against him and sighed happily. "We did. We finally did."

Epilogue

WITH THE HOLIDAYS approaching, and the general state of happiness of his family, Lance didn't feel that the timing was right to share what the private investigator in Aruba had uncovered.

He couldn't involve Asher. He was enjoying being a new father.

Kenzi was a blissful new bride.

Honestly, the lead could be another dead end. Literally.

Or it might be nothing.

All he'd uncovered was the name of a nurse who had also gone missing during the same time frame. What the investigator had found unnerving was how little attention any of the deaths had received either from the authorities or the papers. Either each incident was unrelated or someone very powerful had paid plenty to cover something up.

Ian would think Lance was paranoid if he tried to tell him.

Grant would need more evidence before believing what Lance's gut was beginning to suspect.

Aunt Patrice, were you a sick enough woman to kill your

sister's child? Were you that jealous of her that you'd do anything to hurt her?

Did my mother suspect you? Is that why she had a breakdown?

You ruined my father's career.

How much did you take away from us?

Lance sent a text to the one brother he knew would believe him and who would take the truth with him to the grave if doing so was best for the family. Andrew was deployed on a mission he couldn't discuss, but when following leads that were twenty-eight years old, a few more days or weeks wouldn't make a difference.

Andrew, call me when you get a chance. We need to talk.

THE END

Sign up for my newsletter to hear about upcoming releases and sales:

forms.aweber.com/form/58/1378607658.htm

Coming Soon

Other books by Ruth Cardello

The Legacy Collection:
Also available in audiobook format
Where my billionaires began.

Book 1: Maid for the Billionaire

Book 2: For Love or Legacy

Book 3: Bedding the Billionaire

Book 4: Saving The Sheikh

Book 5: Rise of the Billionaire

Book 6: Breaching the Billionaire: Alethea's Redemption

Book 7: A Corisi Christmas Novella

Novella: Recipe For Love, An Andrade Christmas Novella

The Andrades
Also available in audiobook format
A spin off series of the Legacy Collection with cameos from characters you love from that series.

Book 1: Come Away With Me
Book 2: Home to Me
Book 3: Maximum Risk
Book 4: Somewhere Along the Way
Book 5: Loving Gigi

The Barringtons

A synchronized series. If you love these characters and this world, scroll down for more stories in this world written by other authors. The timelines overlap. The characters flow in and out of each other's books. Each story is a stand alone and the series can be read independently, but they are more fun if you read all three.

Book 1: Always Mine
Book 2: Stolen Kisses
Book 3: Trade It All

Book 4: Let It Burn (Coming 2016)
Book 5: More Than Love (Coming 2017)
Book 6: Forever Now (Coming 2017)
Book 7: Never Goodbye (Coming 2017)

Author Jeannette Winters
Book 1: One White Lie
Book 2: Table for Two
Book 3: You & Me Make Three (Coming July 2016)
Book 4: Virgin for the Fourth Time
Book 5: His for Five Nights
Book 6: After Six

Author Danielle Stewart
Book 1: Fierce Love
Book 2: Wild Eyes
Book 3: Crazy Nights

My characters also appear in Jeannette's Betting on You Series in the Billionaire's Longshot. I loved writing those scenes!
Book 1: The Billionaire's Secret
Book 2: The Billionaire's Masquerade
Book 3: The Billionaire's Longshot
Book 4: The Billionaire's Jackpot
Book 5: All Bets Off

Meet my Cowboys! Lone Star Burn Series:

Hot, fun romances that roam from the country to the city and back.

Book 1: Taken, Not Spurred

Book 2: Tycoon Takedown

Book 3: Taken Home

Book 4: Taking Charge

Looking for spicier?
The Temptation Series:

Guaranteed to put you on Santa's naughty list.

Twelve Days of Temptation and Be My Temptation

Two hot novellas about one sizzling couple.

Other Books:

Taken By a Trillionaire

Ruth Cardello, JS Scott, Melody Anne.

Three hot fantasies about alpha princes and the women who tame them.

About the Author

Ruth Cardello was born the youngest of 11 children in a small city in southern Massachusetts. She spent her young adult years moving as far away as she could from her large extended family. She lived in Boston, Paris, Orlando, New York—then came full circle and moved back to New England. She now happily lives one town over from the one she was born in. For her, family trumped the warmer weather and international scene.

She was an educator for 20 years, the last 11 as a kindergarten teacher. When her school district began cutting jobs, Ruth turned a serious eye toward her second love– writing and has never been happier. When she's not writing, you can find her chasing her children around her small farm, riding her horses, or connecting with her readers online.

Meet my Cowboys! Lone Star Burn Series:

Hot, fun romances that roam from the country to the city and back.

Book 1: Taken, Not Spurred

Book 2: Tycoon Takedown

Book 3: Taken Home

Book 4: Taking Charge

Looking for spicier?
The Temptation Series:

Guaranteed to put you on Santa's naughty list.

Twelve Days of Temptation and Be My Temptation

Two hot novellas about one sizzling couple.

Other Books:

Taken By a Trillionaire

Ruth Cardello, JS Scott, Melody Anne.

Three hot fantasies about alpha princes and the women who tame them.

About the Author

Ruth Cardello was born the youngest of 11 children in a small city in southern Massachusetts. She spent her young adult years moving as far away as she could from her large extended family. She lived in Boston, Paris, Orlando, New York—then came full circle and moved back to New England. She now happily lives one town over from the one she was born in. For her, family trumped the warmer weather and international scene.

She was an educator for 20 years, the last 11 as a kindergarten teacher. When her school district began cutting jobs, Ruth turned a serious eye toward her second love– writing and has never been happier. When she's not writing, you can find her chasing her children around her small farm, riding her horses, or connecting with her readers online.

Contact Ruth:
Website: RuthCardello.com
Email: Minouri@aol.com
FaceBook: Author Ruth Cardello
Twitter: @RuthieCardello

Acknowledgements

I am so grateful to everyone who was part of the process of creating *Trade It All*.

Thank you to:

Nicole Sanders at Trevino Creative Graphic Design for my new cover. You are amazing!

My very patient beta readers. You know who you are. Thank you for kicking my butt when I need it.

My editors: Karen Lawson, Janet Hitchcock, and Marion Archer.

My Roadies for making me smile each day when I log on my computer. So many of you have become friends. Was there life before the Roadies? I'm sure there was, but it wasn't as much fun.

Thank you to my husband, Tony, who is a saint—simple as that

Printed in Great Britain
by Amazon

Printed in Great Britain
by Amazon